Hero Complex

Bluestone Series: Book Three

Isobel Reed

Hero Complex: Bluestone Series: Book Three
Copyright © 2023 Isobel Reed
All rights reserved.

ISBN: (print) 978-1-958136-49-2
(ebook) 978-1-958136-48-5

Inkspell Publishing
207 Moonglow Circle #101
Murrells Inlet, SC 29576

Cover art by: Fantasia Frog Designs
Edited by: Yezanira Venecia

DEDICATION

For my friends- the inspiration and embodiment of the
strong and funny women that I love to write.

CHAPTER ONE

The sun wasn't even up yet, and Ivy was already having an existential crisis. Even the warm, orange glow from the table lamp did nothing to flatter the reflection staring back at her. One thing was for sure though, no matter how long she looked, nothing was going to change anytime soon.

Internally she berated herself. She didn't have time for this. She had chores to do. Horses to feed. And a sexy-as-hell man to try not to humiliate herself in front of.

"Fucking YouTube." She huffed under her breath before dragging herself away from the tilt of her floor-length mirror.

Damn you, Pricilla28! I'm not feeling sexy OR confident. What a load of crap.

There was no time for Ivy to wallow in the YouTube star's betrayal. Or dwell on her poor judgment at trying out a new hair tutorial at stupid o'clock in the morning. Right now, she had things to do. And that meant leaving the confines of her bedroom with her new hairstyle, which was much more male Viking warrior than the sexy, feminine goddess look she was going for.

Damnit all to hell.

Letting out a heavy sigh, Ivy dragged herself and her

manly braid downstairs in search of caffeine. Caffeine wouldn't disappoint her at least. Caffeine was consistent. Reliable. Not at all filled with lies.

With coffee brewed, she was just one sip away from bliss when a loud knock had her cursing again. Back was that funny feeling in her stomach. She knew exactly who was at the door. It had been the same person for the past five days now: Ace. Sweet, kind, thoughtful Ace. Quite possibly the most beautiful man she'd ever seen.

Stop swooning and get it together.

After attempting to plaster on her most neutral, non-swoony facial expression, she made her way through the living room and down the familiar dark-green hallway. A frown momentarily cracking her mask as she took in her surroundings. All this time she'd been worrying about the state of herself instead of the state of her house. What must he think?

Oh, I don't know, maybe that the house is in just as bad shape as everything else in your life?

Ignoring the shockingly loud creak, she flung the front door open and was treated to the best view in town. Her eyes first darted to that perfectly chiseled chest. Thank the Lord for her laundry skills because if she didn't know any better, she was the reason his shirt was currently straining to contain his pecks, and she just couldn't bring herself to be sad about it. Or guilty. She'd done womankind a service, if anything.

When her gaze finally drifted up to the dark stubble dotting his square jaw, it was his intense blue eyes that captured her. She was drowning in them. So much so, it wasn't until Ace cleared his throat that she snapped out of the spell he had her under.

"Mornin', darlin'." There was that deep, smooth Southern drawl that never failed to set butterflies swarming in her stomach. "Can I come in?"

That's about the time she realized she still hadn't said anything.

"Of course. Sorry, sorry. I'm still half asleep. Come in, come in. I've got coffee—well, I just made some. Just this minute. So, you're right on time." Her enthusiasm was verging on manic, but she'd just been caught gawking and desperately needed to distract him from the heat she knew was now darkening her cheeks.

The word vomit continued as she led him past the duct tape-covered couch. "Did you sleep well? I mean, is the cabin okay? It's getting colder now; I'm not sure how warm it's going to be out there this winter. Maybe I could get you some extra blankets. Do you need extra blankets? I'm sure I have some upstairs. Maybe I should go—"

Before she could finish, strong arms spun her around and gripped her biceps. Ace was in her space. His head was dipped, and his mouth was just a breath away from her. How was she supposed to form coherent sentences now? And that smell. Sweet baby Jesus. He smelt like sandalwood and sunshine.

"Darlin', you need to take a breath. What's going on with you today? And what the hell happened to your hair?"

If her cheeks weren't red before, they were definitely flaming now. Quickly scrambling out of his hold, she fumbled with her braid, clumsily untying it until a mass of messy brown hair hung over her shoulders.

"I was trying something new, that's all. It was much harder than it looked online, if you must know. I'm sorry you're so offended by it!"

Closing the distance between them, his large finger skimmed her chin until he'd tilted it upward. That was when she once again found herself staring into those deep blue pools. "Sugar, it's not you, that's all. I wasn't tryin' to be rude. You're finer than a frog's hair split four ways. You don't need nothing doing to that pretty little head of yours."

What the hell does that mean?

It was bad enough she looked a mess. Now, she felt like one too. Taking a step back, she attempted a shaky smile. He'd rattled her. He was always rattling her. With his weird compliments and intense, longer-than-socially-acceptable eye contact. Great. Now her palms were sweating. She'd officially hit her humiliation limit for the day, and it wasn't even 5:30 yet. Coffee. She needed coffee.

Turning her back on the big, beautiful man before her, she scurried over to the kitchen. Although she heard him follow behind her, she decided it was best for everyone if she avoided looking at him directly in the eyes for the foreseeable future. Who knew what else was going to come out of her mouth or how much redder she could get?

After pouring a mug of the good stuff for him, she expertly handed it over without meeting his gaze. She was doing so well. Until she wasn't. Apparently, grazing his hand was just too much for her and her long-neglected hormones. Her hand instinctively jerked at the feel of his touch.

Perfect. He thinks I'm a freak. A jumpy, babbling, sweaty, red freak with bad hair. Is it time for the earth to swallow me whole yet?

She refused to meet his eyes and luckily, he didn't call her on it. Instead, they both drank in silence. Awkward silence. This was not how she wanted today to go. It wasn't as if she thought Ace would fall at her feet when he got a look at her goddess braid, but she was hoping for something. And whatever that frog thing was, it definitely wasn't it. That was just him being his normal polite, if a little weird, self.

She was just about sick of polite. Ace was the embodiment of polite. He was all good manners, appropriate conversations, and good old-fashioned chivalry. But something was missing. He was holding something back. Granted, she hadn't known him all that long, but she had a feeling this version of him hadn't always been his default setting.

They'd met just a month ago at Local Deputy Brady Mitchell's house. She'd been there to visit his wife, Alice, and stumbled across the reunion. Ace was an old friend who had served with Brady and was in need of a place to stay. Obviously lust-drunk at the time, Ivy offered up one of the empty ranch cabins at Moonrock. It wasn't like she needed them anymore. She'd recently had to let her last ranch hand go. She was barely making enough money to feed herself, let alone anyone else.

In only a week of having Ace there, Ivy was smitten. Actually, if she were being honest with herself, she was smitten a month ago. In exchange for his stay, he'd instantly offered up his services, and despite her thorough protests, she was secretly happy to have the help.

"What's got you thinking so hard?" Breaking the silence, he reached out and covered her hand with his.

If she thought Ace's earlier finger graze was too much, the hand covering definitely had it beat. Easily. Instead of a jerk, this time, her body chose violence. A second later, the white ceramic mug she had been clutching onto was shattered and chunky pieces of it were now surrounding her feet.

"Mother-effing sugar balls!"

Ace just laughed. He didn't seem fazed at all. Or even slightly shocked. Maybe she just looked like the kind of woman who smashed mugs on the regular and he'd already mentally prepared for the possibility.

In true take charge, Ace fashion, he instructed her to "not move a muscle" and casually sauntered toward the kitchen sink cupboards in search of a dustpan.

Don't stare at his ass. Don't stare at his ass. Don't stare at his ass.

Despite her optimistic chant, her eyes were, in fact, glued to his ass. And they stayed there even when he bent down to peer inside the lower cabinet. The way those Wranglers clung to his behind was practically obscene. And she loved it. So much so, she couldn't seem to drag her eyes away.

Unfortunately, stealthy was not her middle name. At some point in between Ace bending over and him actually finding the dustpan, she'd found herself trapped in a lust-fuelled trance. Which was why she didn't seem to notice him straighten and turn around. Not until her eyes and his crotch were formally introduced, that is.

Dear Lord.

Quickly darting her gaze back up to safer territory, she realized instantly that she'd been caught. The man was smirking at her.

Well done, Ivy. You should get some sort of award. Breaking the record for most embarrassing moments before the sun has even risen.

She watched in silence as he swept up the mess. She could no longer trust herself. It was going to be a long day.

***

It was safe to say she had not learned her lesson from earlier, because the best part of mucking out the stalls was definitely Ace bending over. She decided to justify it by reasoning that good things in her life right now were few and far between. So, she needed to take pleasure in the little things. Or the perfectly shaped things, wrapped in denim.

Dear Lord, it's like it's been carved out by the Gods themselves.

Was she shamelessly ogling Ace's ass? Yes. Was it worth potentially being a defendant in a sexual harassment in the workplace lawsuit? Yes. It was.

"What are you doing?" Ace's booming voice brought her back to reality.

Shit. Busted. Again.

"Uh, um, nothing. I just … I just remembered I need to put in a new feed order today. I was trying to think of everything we need." *Lies.*

Ace's lips twitched. "Well, I'm glad my ass reminded you of that, sugar."

Red. I'm bright red. I know it.

Averting her eyes, Ivy dipped her head and went back to the task at hand, ignoring Ace's chuckles beside her.

She didn't know what it was about Ace that turned her into this person. Who even was this person? She hardly even recognized herself. There was just something about him that made her want to impress him. But needless to say, it really wasn't working.

Then there was the blushing. What was with all the blushing? Before he turned up, she couldn't even remember when she'd last blushed. But now? Now, she looked like she was permanently sporting a face full of sunburn.

Fuck my life.

It was only when it came time to take the horses for a ride that she started to relax again. This was her favorite part of the day.

After saddling up the newest addition to her family, Justice, she rode up beside Ace, who was waiting for her on Blaze, then they set off across the pasture.

The sun was finally making itself known. She enjoyed every second of the spotted heat absorbing into her skin. With the new season upon them, the morning air was beginning to cool. It was only a matter of time before the mud softened and the rich greens burnt amber.

"You're extra quiet today, sugar. Something on your mind?" Ace's husky drawl sent a shiver down her spine. She loved it when he called her *sugar*.

There was something on her mind. In fact, it felt like there was always something on her mind lately. Niggling her. Worrying her. Keeping her up at night. Things at Moonrock had been rough for a while. And with everything falling onto her shoulders, it was starting to weigh her down.

Other than her only brother, Teddy, she was alone. Teddy liked to joke that he didn't have the ranching gene. But, really, horse breeding just wasn't his passion, not like it was for Ivy. And that was okay. He'd left school and gone straight into the Navy, and she couldn't be prouder. Since retiring, he preferred the social aspect of working behind the bar at Mickey's, the only bar in Bluestone.

As close as they were, she tried not to bother him with the issues the ranch was having. He wasn't stupid though. He'd been injecting cash into the business for years. Insisting that since he didn't contribute physically, it was only right that he helped out financially. And if it wasn't for that money, Moonrock would have been closed long ago. One thing was for sure, though, her brother wouldn't be able to bail her out forever. Something had to change. Soon.

"Just the usual, Ace, nothing for you to worry about."

"The usual?"

She peeked over at him long enough to see his bushy brown eyebrow raised in her direction. "Yeah, the usual. My business to-do lists."

"Anything I can help with?"

Seriously, this man was something else. Wasn't he already doing enough? The fact she wasn't even paying him for his labor was bad enough. They both knew the work he was doing was worth much more than free accommodation in a tiny shack. As if she'd ask him for anything else.

"No, Ace, if anything you're doing way too much. I already told you the cabin is yours for as long as you want it … You really don't need to help me every day. There must be plenty of other things you'd rather be doing than mucking out stalls." She glanced over her shoulder at him to make sure he heard and was met with a panty-dropping smile. Jesus.

"Believe it or not, there's no place I'd rather be." He ignored her very unladylike snort and continued. "Now … you gonna tell me what's really going on?"

Feeling extra stubborn, Ivy not-so-subtly brushed him off again. "Um … no, I don't think I will if it's all the same."

"Ivy," he warned, his voice all rumbly, "seriously."

"It's no big deal, Ace. Really."

"If it's no big deal, then you shouldn't mind telling me, sugar."

"Why are you pushing this?"

"Why don't you wanna tell me?

"You always answer a question with a question?" Ivy clipped back.

His smile widened. "Not always. You always try and deflect when you don't want to answer a question?"

Damn. He had her there. Well, fine. If he wanted the

truth, she'd give him the truth. Let the man feel sorry for her if that's what he wanted. It wasn't like things could get more awkward between them than they already were.

Why the hell not? Someone other than my punching pillow should hear it anyway.

"Fine, you want to know what's up, I'll tell you." Ivy huffed haughtily. She tugged at Justice's reigns and brought them to a stop and waited for Ace to follow suit.

When she turned to face him, she saw the concern furrowing his brow.

"It's no secret Moonrock is failing. And as the lucky owner and sole employee … I've got some tough decisions to make. Crappy ones. Like really, really crappy ones." Her hand automatically went to Justice's smooth, coffee-colored mane. Just the feel of him soothed her. Well, until she remembered Donoghue. "And I-I have a meeting this afternoon. An important one. And I really need it to go well. I can't mess it up. Well, I'm going to try really hard to not to mess it up."

Ace was now full-blown frowning. "What makes you think you'll mess it up?"

"Well, for one, it's with Mr. Donoghue, who by the way, is scary as hell. Think Voldemort meets Mr. Burns. And he's kind of a big deal in the industry. Oh, and I have no idea what he wants. He used to be a client—a long time ago—but he only ever dealt with Pops. I'm really hoping he wants to breed some of his mares. To have him back as a client would be huge for Moonrock. As in, it could be the difference between me closing the ranch doors in a few months. I'm just nervous I guess. That's all. I'm sure it will be fine. And if not, I'll think of something else."

She went back to stroking Justice, hoping like hell it really would be all right. When she glanced back up, Ace had a serious expression on his face. His blue eyes were boring into her. She could have sworn she saw the color switch from light to dark.

"How 'bout I go with you?"

She instinctively shook her head. "No. You don't need to do that." Ace really had done enough.

"What if I want to?"

"No one *wants* to have coffee with the dark lord, Ace."

He flashed her that dazzling smile again. "No, I'm sure they don't. But I'd bet they'd sure like to have coffee with the beautiful woman sitting across from me."

Oh, Lord have mercy.

CHAPTER TWO

Ace supposed that agreeing to spend the afternoon with Ivy wasn't exactly keeping his distance, but it wasn't like he was doing all that well anyway. Avoiding her was much easier when he was staying at Brady's. Now he was at Moonrock, and in less than a week, he'd officially become an Ivy addict.

There was just something about her. Something that brought out some archaic caveman instinct to protect and help. And possess.

Chill, man. You sound like some sort of deranged stalker.

Ace knew deep down the whole "possess" thing wasn't exactly healthy. Maybe he just wanted to call her his? Yes. That sounds better. More socially acceptable. He wanted her. That was all.

A year ago, he would have just asked her out. But a lot can happen in a year. Like, say, a car bomb explodes and leaves you with burns covering half of your upper body and face. And your life as a marine, the only career you've ever known or wanted, comes to an abrupt end when you're medically discharged. Then, as if all those changes weren't enough, you leave behind your home in Texas and move across the country to escape the never-ending pity that awaits around every corner of your hometown.

Talk about starting again. If he was honest, though, twelve months in this new body had been the biggest adjustment of them all. It was hard to look in the mirror some days. His doctors told him that it would get easier. Eventually. But who knows? The fact was, if he couldn't look at himself, why the hell would anyone else want to?

He side-glanced Ivy again. She was muttering to herself as she white-knuckled the steering wheel. Something about a Pricilla. She was cute as hell when she was all flustered. When they'd first met, she'd been shy, but somehow he knew there was a firecracker lurking just beneath the surface. He was pleased to see that side of her slowly making an appearance.

"What?" Ivy asked, catching him looking over.

"Who's Pricilla?" He felt his smile widen as a flush began to creep up her neck.

"A liar," she muttered under her breath as she parked up along Bluestone's main street.

That was another thing about Ivy he liked. She said it like it was, but was careful never to be mean. If she thought the truth wasn't appropriate, she would say very little or nothing at all. Knowing all this, he didn't push for any further information. He didn't need to. It was already clear that whoever this Pricilla was, she was on Ivy's shit list.

As they walked along the cobbled sidewalk, he found himself resisting a very strong urge to grab Ivy's hand. Which was insane. They weren't dating. They were friends. And he needed to remind himself of that. Over and over again apparently.

Keep it together, man.

He'd never experienced anything like the pull he felt toward her. It wasn't just a superficial attraction that had his blood heating either. There was no doubt she was beautiful. He'd have to be blind not to notice. But it was more than that. Who she was on the inside was shining out of those sparkling green eyes, forcing him to take notice.

Three doors down, he held open the door of Beano's, Bluestone's finest coffee shop, and followed Ivy inside. Instinctively his hand went to the small of her back as he guided her through the tables and toward the counter. He expertly ignored the spark as his fingertips innocently grazed her back and, instead, he focused on the nutty coffee aroma now filling his lungs. *Nice.*

This was his first time in Beano's, and he liked it already. The chunky wooden furniture more than made up for the very hipster exposed brick walls. He even liked the low-hanging lights.

Before they'd made it to the counter, an older, slightly plump man stood. This must be the infamous Donoghue. He didn't exactly look like a supervillain, but Ace had to admit, the man was giving off bad vibes. Vibes Ivy obviously picked up on too, as she flinched beneath his hand.

It looked as though his and Ivy's drink order would have to wait. Changing direction, they made their way over to Donoghue's table. As expected, the man gave Ace a thorough once-over, and he was suddenly glad he'd changed into clean Wranglers and a flannel shirt that fit him better than the one Ivy had shrunk. Predictably, Donoghue's gaze lingered on Ace's burns.

Yep. I'm a freakshow, I get it.

Finally shifting his attention away from Ace, Donoghue greeted Ivy with a stiff nod and proceeded to sit back down. Ace scooted a chair closer to Ivy before he joined them. She was nervous, shaking one leg erratically. Before he could stop himself, his hand stilled her and rested on her thigh. Instead of stiffening beneath his touch or shooting him daggers, he watched her slowly sink into her seat. He did it. He helped calm her. Why did that feel so good?

"Nice to see you again, Mr. Donoghue. This is Ace." She gestured over to him with a dainty hand, then turned back to Ace and offered him up the brightest smile he'd ever seen. "Ace, this is Mr. Donoghue."

Still absorbing that smile, Ace almost missed Donoghue's outstretched hand. Almost.

"Ace, pleasure." Was it though? By the hard line of his mouth, Ace didn't quite believe the man.

"Now, Ivy, I bet you're wondering why I asked you to meet with me today."

Ivy visibly brightened, clearly not reading the room. "Yes, well, I figured it was about Justice. I've not had him very long, but I can assure you he's one of the best studs I've ever owned and just perfect for your mares."

Ace watched on as the graying man cleared his throat. Ace knew right then what was coming next wasn't going to be good.

"I've not heard about Justice, Ivy. In fact, no one has. And there lies the issue. Your business is failing. I hate to say it, but ever since your grandfather passed away, you've run that place into the ground."

Ivy's gasp immediately made him want to smash the asshat's face in, right there and then. But Donoghue didn't seem to sense the imminent danger and carried on.

"Look, I know this world, and I share the same concerns as other clients you've no doubt lost. A little thing like you is better suited to handling the admin side of the business and leaving the running of things to a man. Men work better with other men. I'm not being sexist, it's just a fact. Now, it would be a different story if you were married and your husband was taking care of things, but you're not."

Hang on, did he just say that Ivy is losing clients because she's an unmarried woman? What the actual fuck?

Every muscle on Ace tensed, his hand had even drawn back from Ivy's thigh so he had enough room to clench it into a fist. Just as he was readying to tell this arrogant, sexist prick where to go, Ivy surprised him. Straightening in her chair, her voice remained calm but firm.

"Mr. Donoghue, somehow I very much doubt you've come here just to enlighten me as to all the reasons you will not be doing business with me. As my patience is wearing exceptionally thin, if you have a point, I suggest you get to it."

Donoghue's gray eyes narrowed on her. "Yes, Ivy, you're correct; I do have a point. I know the bank manager over in Splitrock, and he may have let slip that you're behind on your loans. Now, as a favor to your grandfather, I'm willing to pay off the bank loans and take over the ranch. I'll also make sure you have enough money to buy a house here in town."

Is this guy for real?

"As a favor to my grandfather?" Ivy screeched. Way less calm now. In fact, there may be ringing in his ears. "Wow. You have some nerve, Mr. Donoghue. How dare you?" Ivy rose from her chair, those pretty pink cheeks turning scarlet as she stared down at the gray-haired cowboy, "You know what you can do with your favor?" Ace had an idea. "You can take your *oh-so-noble* favor and shove it where the sun don't shine."

Yes, Ivy.

Even through his anger, Ace couldn't help but smile. She was tough as hell.

Donoghue's face was just as red as Ivy's as he shot up from his seat. "You're making a mistake, missy. My offer is more than fair, and you know it. You're alone and up to your eyes in debt. You'll be lucky to squeeze a penny out of that ranch before the bank seizes it."

Ace didn't know why he said what he said next. Maybe it was that word "alone," or maybe it was that pesky caveman inside rearing its ugly head again. Whatever it was, he knew there would be consequences. And yet, he obviously didn't care enough to stop himself.

"You're wrong. She's not alone. She has me. Her *fiancé*. So spread the word far and wide—Moonrock is not for sale."

When he went to grab Ivy's hand, she was just staring at him, mouth wide open. "Come on, sugar, let's blow this pop stand." He laced his fingers through hers and practically dragged her out of there.

He faintly heard some gasps from the other patrons. Donoghue clearly hadn't been the only one to hear Ace's announcement. He'd worry about that later. Neither of them looked back as they hit the sidewalk, but Ace's heart was beating so fast, he was a little concerned it would break through his ribs any second now.

Fiancé? Jesus Christ. Where the hell did that come from?

As they walked back to Ivy's truck, Ace still couldn't quite believe he'd just announced to half of Bluestone that they were engaged. And if the silence was anything to go by, neither could Ivy.

It wasn't until they were safely buckled in that she finally spoke. "I can't believe you just did that."

Neither can I.

"It just came out. The shit he said about you being alone. It pissed me off. You're not alone. You have me."

Ivy stared at him a moment. He watched her gulp. "This will be all over town by the end of the day, you know that, right? Everyone is gonna think we're engaged." Her hands quickly covered her face, hiding it from view as she continued. "Oh my God, they're gonna think I'm pregnant. That you knocked me up! Why else would you propose to someone you met a month ago?" She was babbling again; she did this when she was flustered, and it was adorable. "What are we gonna do? God. Maybe I can call Teddy. Yeah, that's it. I'll call Teddy. I'll tell him what happened and get him to start spreading the word that it's not true. He knows everyone in town. Yep. Okay. That's what I'll do."

As she reached for her phone, Ace quickly clamped his big hand over it. "Don't." It occurred to him right then that he'd done this on purpose. His brain just hadn't caught up with his mouth until now. "I think it's best to let people think we're together."

"What? Why?" Her face was a picture of horror.

Yeah, of course she's horrified. Look in the mirror. The last thing she wants is for people to think she's marrying Freddy Kruger.

"If what Donoghue said was true, that your clients are sexist assholes, then I guess we should probably test that theory. Now that there's a man in the picture, maybe we can see about getting some of your old business back."

"And what makes you think I want to work with those sexist A-holes?"

"To save Moonrock," he stated plainly. "Come on, Ivy. What other options do you have? Let's take their money, save the ranch, and then concentrate on getting better clients. Yeah?"

The longer she pondered, the more his stomach twisted. He was really doing this. Shockingly, he really wanted to do this. For her. For the ranch. She deserved everything. If he could give her this, help save the business she loved so much, he'd die a happy man. He knew it.

After what felt like forever, she let out a sigh and turned to him.

"You're right. I'm out of ideas. Okay. Let's do this."

Why the hell was he so damn excited?

Sick. You're sick. A glutton for fucking punishment.

***

"Word around town is you're engaged. Congratulations, buddy!"

Ace watched on as Brady almost doubled over with laughter.

Great. Now I'm being mocked in my own damn home.

"You about done, Mitchell?" Ace pinched the bridge of his nose in the vain hope it might dispel some of the newfound tension making its way up his body.

It didn't work.

It also didn't magically gift him with patience. So he retreated back inside the cabin, not surprised as his friend followed behind him, still laughing his ass off.

A bit like the old house Ivy lived in, the cabin had seen better days. It didn't really have much of a kitchen, but it did have a small corner sectioned off that he assumed was supposed to be one. In it was a countertop portable stove, a sink, and a mini fridge. It suited him just fine, though. Ramen was his specialty.

Grabbing two bottles of beer from the fridge, he took his time untwisting the caps and handing one over to Brady, who had now, thankfully, recovered from his convulsions.

"So, you gonna tell me what the hell is going on?" His friend raised a brow as he took his first swig.

"It's a long story, brother."

"Good thing I ain't got nothing but time." As if to prove that point, Brady bounced down onto Ace's leather couch.

After letting out a sigh, Ace supposed it was a good idea to talk to someone about the predicament he'd found himself in. Brady was his best friend and practically a brother to him, so Ace already knew he could trust him.

The couch was too small to contain them both, so Ace dragged over a stool and settled in to tell the story of Donoghue, the bank, and the ranch.

When he was done, he wasn't surprised to see that his friend was just as upset as he was.

"Jesus, man, I had no idea how much Ivy was struggling. And I know for a fact she's not told Ali, either."

"She's tough as hell, doing all this on her own. I reckon it all boils down to pride for her." Ace still didn't know how she'd managed to keep the ranch afloat for as long as she had and all on her own, but he was beyond impressed at her strength.

"So, what, you're just gonna pretend you're her fiancé and try and get her some clients? How long is that gonna take?"

"No idea, but it's not like I'm doing anything else, man. I'm good for money—fifteen years of being a marine has left me with some decent savings. Plus, I got my payout after my medical discharge."

Brady only grunted in response. The Marine Corps was a sore subject for them both. They'd expected to be career military. There was no way they ever thought they'd be medically discharged like they were.

"She's a nice girl." *And beautiful and sweet and funny and sexy as hell.* Ace kept those particular thoughts to himself. "I want to help her. And I like working here, even if it's just for free board. It gives me something to do. I got a lot of energy to burn right now."

"I get it, man, but people ain't stupid. You've been in Bluestone a month. Don't you think it looks a bit odd that you're now engaged?"

"Well, you obviously heard the gossip. Sounds to me that people believe it enough to spread it. I reckon we can spin that whole whirlwind romance thing, and don't forget I am living here. Hell, maybe I'll even move into the main house with her to make it more convincing."

Now there was an idea.

Brady stared at him a while, his dark eyes narrowing on Ace suspiciously. "Don't do it, man. She's a nice girl."

"*I'm* the one who said she's a nice girl, brother. And don't do what?" Ace may feign innocence, but he knew exactly what Brady was talking about.

Ace looked on as his friend dragged his hand through his dark hair. "You know exactly what I'm talking about. Ivy's a good woman, who's had it rough. She lost her parents young. Her and Teddy were brought up by their grandparents, and now they're gone too. She's not the kind of chick you mess with. You wanna get your rocks off, look elsewhere. Understand?"

It was fair to say Ace wasn't a relationship kind of guy. Something Brady obviously knew, hence the warning. But that isn't to say Ace wasn't capable of a relationship. That he didn't want one. Being a marine meant he was never in the same place for very long. That was why being in a relationship didn't make any sense to him. What was the point when you would spend more time away from each other than together?

Ace held his palms up defensively. "I fucking know that,

23

man. Jesus. You really think that little of me, huh? I told you I think she's a nice girl. The last thing I wanna do is mess with her. And yes, that includes doing a hit and run."

That much was true. He also didn't think he'd have a chance in hell in getting Ivy into his bed. It had been a long time since he'd been with anyone, even before the car bomb took away his one asset: his looks. He doubted any woman would want him now. Especially not someone as special as Ivy.

"Okay. Just making sure you don't hurt her, man, that's all. 'Cause if you did, you should know, Ali would have no problem kicking your ass." Brady smirked and placed his empty bottle on the chunky coffee table. "Look, word of advice. You'll probably wanna talk to her brother, Teddy, man to man. He's a good guy but protective as hell of his sister, and right now he thinks you're engaged to her. And I doubt he's happy about that."

Damn. Brady was right. Ace had only met Teddy in passing at the bar. He needed to introduce himself, properly. Formally.

"Oh, and you should know … he's a former SEAL."

Fuck.

"What?"

"A SEAL, dude, so watch your back." Brady chuckled.

Ace was glad someone found this funny.

CHAPTER THREE

"What the hell do you mean you're moving in?" Ivy's mouth hung open.

Just a few hours a day with Ace was hard enough. Spending twenty-four-seven with him was bound to make her break out in hives. Pretending to be perfect was becoming harder and harder as it was. There was no way she could keep that up if he moved in.

Ace stood in the doorway, unfazed by the horror she was doing a piss poor job of hiding. "Like I said, Ivy, I'm moving in. And tomorrow I'm gonna start contacting some of your old clients, see if I can get some meetings set up."

Ivy blinked a few too many times as she tried to process what Ace was saying. "And why the hell did you assume that I'd be okay with you moving in? That I'd be okay with you contacting *my* clients?" It was either panic or rage making her voice crack. She hadn't decided yet.

"Sugar …" His voice was annoyingly calm. "Remember when we announced to the town that we were engaged?"

"You mean when *you* announced to the town we were engaged?"

One corner of his mouth lifted into a crooked smile, and damn if that wasn't the sexiest thing she'd ever seen.

"Yeah, darlin', when *I* announced it, and *you* agreed to go along with it. Well, as your new fiancé, don't you think it makes more sense for me to live here with you? I meant what I said, Ivy. I want to help. You just need to let me."

She felt her shoulders slouch as she thought about what lay ahead of her. She did need help, but she wasn't great at accepting it.

As if sensing her reluctance, Ace took a step toward her. In one swift motion, his callused hand was cupping her face and his thumb was gently caressing her. That simple touch managed to steal all the air out of her lungs.

"I promise we can fix this together. You just have to trust me, okay? Can you do that?"

In all honesty, it was hard to speak with his thumb caressing her cheek like it was, let alone commit to trust. "I … I … uh, I don't know. I'm used to doing all this stuff by myself."

"Well, you don't have to anymore. You've got me."

He kept saying that. But for how long? She knew it wouldn't be long until he was gone too. Just like everyone else.

"Have you got some kind of hero complex or something? Do you always go around helping damsels in distress, or am I a special case?" She gazed into those intense blue eyes. She didn't know what she was searching for, but she was certain there was something hidden away there.

"Oh, you're a special case all right, sugar."

Suddenly her mouth was drier than the desert, and her heart was about ready to break through her chest. If she wasn't blushing already, there was no doubt she'd be beetroot in a matter of seconds. What the hell was going on? No other man had ever affected her like this.

Get your shit together, Ivy. You're a thirty-year-old woman, damnit, not some dumb teenager with a crush.

Was she really going to do this? Let this beautiful man move in with her? Let him see what a dork she really was? How utterly imperfect she was?

Her body was apparently more than on board with the idea. Before her brain could stop her, she was widening the gap between herself and the door and allowing him entry.

Goddamnit. He must have hypnotized me with that thumb-stroke thing.

"Uh, I guess you can stay in the spare bedroom."

Ace's smile widened until the puckered marks on his face creased. "I take it that means you're gonna accept my help."

Looking down at the floor, she hoped she didn't look as helpless as she felt. "I don't think I have a choice."

***

It was safe to say Ace moving in with her was not going well. Actually, it was going really freaking badly. This morning was a prime example of why she should've never agreed to his dumbass plan.

With only one bathroom, it was the second time this week that she'd inadvertently run into him coming out of the shower. It wasn't that she didn't enjoy seeing Ace half naked, she really did. It was his reaction to her, which was a real sucker punch to the stomach. The man couldn't get away from her fast enough. She could have sworn she saw skid marks.

It was early afternoon, and she was still nursing her bruised ego. To make matters worse, she was currently fighting the urge to smack Thomas Weston across his stupid smug face. The former client and card-carrying sexist pig apparently prefers to direct all his questions to a penis, in this case, Ace. So rather than, you know, ask the actual ranch owner and altogether the most frigging qualified person in the damn room, Weston was only talking to Ace.

Don't scream. Don't scream. Don't scream.

To his credit, Ace knew a lot more about the business than she imagined, but it was still really annoying. The other really annoying thing was his hand on her thigh. It was distracting. Confusing. How was she supposed to continue shooting daggers at Weston when the warmth of Ace's touch was comforting her and mocking her at the same time?

Ace had made it abundantly clear over the past few days that he was not interested in her, which made having his hands on her even more perplexing. Since he'd moved in, it was like they had reversed roles. He was the one avoiding eye contact now, and even the slightest graze or touch from her would send the man running for the hills. It wasn't exactly doing wonders for her self-esteem.

"Have you set a date?" Thomas's question dragged her out of her inner turmoil.

"Not yet"—Ace squeezed her thigh as he spoke, causing her to actually quiver—"but I'm hoping it will be sooner rather than later."

Ivy just smiled. She figured that in Thomas's world, women were merely silent, pretty objects. Which worked in her favor, as she certainly didn't have anything to say to the douchecanoe.

"Well, it's wonderful to see you finally settling down, Ivy. You've got yourself a good man here. One who will no doubt do your grandfather's legacy justice."

Another tight smile, teamed with a small nod, as she pictured strangling him with his own tacky belt.

Ace must have sensed she was nearing her limit because he wrapped up quickly after that and escorted Thomas back to his truck, leaving Ivy to pace her office. Straighten some stacks of papers. She even organized the pens in order of color. Anything to distract herself from how dirty she felt. She was doing business with the devil.

"Well, that went better than expected." Ace's rumbly voice halted the pacing she'd defaulted to. "He's committed to two mares."

That was good news. It really was. So why wasn't she jumping for joy?

"It just feels wrong. All of it. What happens when this"—she motioned between the two of them—"stops being a thing? He's just gonna drop me again. And he's such a … such a …"

Ace's lips twitched. "Such a what?"

"Such a fucking pig. A big, giant, condescending, sexist pig."

Damnit. Even Ace's laugh was sexy. Smoother than a shot of whiskey.

"I think that's the first time I've heard you curse. I kinda like it."

"You do?" The question just slipped out and hadn't hidden her surprise. She'd been trying extra hard not to curse in front of Ace. She figured it was just another part of her that was imperfect and needed hiding.

Ace stalked toward her and waited until he was just inches away before tucking an errant strand of hair behind her ear. "I do." The familiar scent of sandalwood hit the back of her throat as his smoldering gaze held her in place. "There's an awful lot I like about you, sugar." Those sneaky fingers of his left scorch marks as he lightly ran them down her cheek and along her jaw.

This man was giving her whiplash. He'd spent days avoiding her like a bad smell, and now he was in her space, treating her to hot flashes.

A not-so-subtle "ahem" had their connection severed. Now that Ace wasn't blocking her vision, she could see Luke slouched in the doorway.

"Hey, sorry, Luke, thank you for coming at such short notice."

"No problem, Ivy." Luke treated her to that dazzling pearly white smile. "Anything for you."

Ivy snorted. "Ever the charmer, Luke. Come on, let's go take a look at Blaze."

Making her way over, she spared a look in Ace's direction and was surprised to see he was scowling. Like actual scowling. There might even have been a low growl thing happening at the back of his throat. Good. Maybe being jealous will help him pull his head out of his ass.

She didn't bother introducing the two men and gestured for Luke to follow her. Yes, she was being petty, but she didn't care. She deserved some petty. Small joys and all that.

***

Ivy was nervous. She'd never once lied to her brother. Not a major lie anyway. There was this one time when she accidentally stepped on his most prized video game, and she had no other choice but to blame it on their dog, Buster. But apart from that, she was pretty much the embodiment of a perfect sister.

As she waited in the far corner of Mickey's for Teddy's bar shift to end, she contemplated telling him the truth. It was true that he would understand why she was doing it, but he wouldn't like it. He would try and convince her to sell the ranch again, and she really didn't want a repeat of that conversation. So, theoretically, this should be easier.

Her gaze flicked back to Teddy, who was pulling yet another pint. He had on his usual easy smile as he charmed the patrons. Sometimes she wished she could borrow a smidgen of that charm. Maybe it would help her cling onto her remaining clients.

Just when she thought she couldn't be any more tense, the last person she wanted to see pushed his way into the bar: Ace. He was shortly followed by Brady and Ali. They hadn't spotted her though. She was tucked into a darkened corner, and they were headed straight to the bar. *No, no, no.* She needed to intercept. Like, right now. Other than confirming their relationship to her brother, she hadn't had a chance to explain yet. So there was a good chance Ace was in danger.

Barrelling toward the steel-topped bar, in a less-than-graceful fashion, she immediately positioned herself in between Ace and Teddy.

"Well, hello, darlin." Ace's head dipped until his mouth was hovering just over her ear. "I thought it'd be a good idea to have a little chat with your brother, you know, man to man. Now that I'm your fiancé and all."

Ignore the goosebumps. There are no goosebumps. Goosebumps do not exist.

Ace's big hands wrapped around her and settled over her stomach. She resisted the urge to suck in her belly. Because it definitely didn't matter. Nope. In fact, neither did the feel of his abnormally hard chest. Or the amount of heat radiating off him that may or may not result in her back setting alight. And if all that wasn't fun enough, she then had to somehow not spontaneously combust as she felt his hot breath all over her as he continued to whisper into her ear.

"It's gonna be okay, sugar. I promise. Trust me, remember?"

She was pretty certain a whimper escaped her lips. That probably didn't help the situation. Not when she met Teddy's green-eyed glare, who looked about ready to jump over the bar and flatten Ace. To be fair, Teddy probably would and could. What with being a former SEAL and all.

"Table now." That direct order from Teddy was to Ivy.

Her brother pushed back on the bar top and headed toward the table Ivy had picked out earlier. As she went to obey and follow behind, Ace kept her in place, his arms tightening their grip around her.

She could feel him turn his head above her as he addressed Brady and Alice. "We'll catch up with you guys later—we gotta go talk to Teddy for a bit."

We? Oh hell no.

Seeing as Ace wasn't about to let her go anytime soon, Ivy twisted in his embrace until they were face to face, still pressed into each other. She didn't think this through. There was literally no air between them. Where was all the air?

"Sugar?"

Oh, yeah. Right. Snap out of it, Ivy.

"I think I need to speak to him alone. For now. How 'bout I join you guys in a bit when I'm done?"

"No can do, sugar, not when he's got his tail up like that." He loosened his grip slightly and let his hands travel to her waist.

"He's my brother, Ace; what exactly do you think he's gonna do?" The man was exasperating and still too damn close.

"Yeah, and I'm your man … technically. So, we do this together."

Her dramatic groan quickly turned into a sigh as she tried to untangle herself.

"Fine." She huffed. Even though she was now free from his hold, Ace hadn't let her get very far. He'd immediately taken the opportunity to tuck her into his side and guided her back toward the dark corner. "Just try not to piss him off, okay?"

Ace simply sniggered and dropped a kiss on top of her head. That was not an answer.

Teddy was already seated when they arrived at the back. And still glaring. If looks could kill, Ace would be a goner.

This should be fun.

"So"—Teddy crossed his burly arms over his chest—"you gonna explain to me why I had to hear about my little sister's engagement from Dotty?"

Ivy shifted on the hard wooden chair. It made sense that Dotty found out first. She owned and worked in the only diner in Bluestone. The heart of the gossip mill as it were.

"Teddy, I'm—"

"It's my fault," Ace cut her off. "I don't think we've been formally introduced. I'm Ace." Ace offered his hand, but Teddy didn't take it. He was too mad.

"I know who you are. You served with Brady. A marine. And, apparently, lacking in basic fucking manners. You're just now introducing yourself, huh? After shacking up with my sister for a month and somehow convincing her to marry you."

Ivy spared a glance at Ace just in time to see his jaw tick. *Oh dear.* You could cut the tension around the table with a knife. Not knowing quite what to say, she slurped on her whiskey Coke. If there were ever a time to drink, it would be now.

"Are you pregnant? That why you marrying him? He knocked you up?"

She almost choked on her drink. Maybe slurping wasn't the best idea.

"No, Teddy, he hasn't *knocked me up*, as you so eloquently put it."

"That the only reason you think she'd marry a man like me, huh?" Ace chimed in.

"Damn straight." Teddy rose and so did Ace. Great. Now they were posturing.

Ivy stayed seated but with one sharp tug pulled Ace down until he was sat beside her again.

"All right, all right. Calm the hell down. You guys about done with your dick-measuring contest?" Nothing but grunts. "Look, Teddy, I'm really sorry you had to find out that way. Really, I am. I agree; you should've heard it from me—from us. But I can't go back in time and change that. All I can do is apologize."

She watched as her brother slowly lowered himself back down into his seat. She was getting through. Thank God. "Ace and I are together. I'm not pregnant, and he's not a douchebag. You guys actually have a lot in common, and if you give him a chance, I'm sure you could be friends. But if not, I need you to accept the fact that we're together. Respect it. Please. For me."

Teddy met her eyes and hopefully recognized the silent pleading. He didn't say anything for a moment, just darted his gaze between Ace and her.

"You hurt her and I'll fucking end you. Do you understand me, Marine?"

Ace simply scoffed, but thankfully didn't rise to it. "I'd rather hurt myself than her. Believe that, Navy boy."

CHAPTER FOUR

Luke was sniffing around again. Goddamn smug bastard. With those fake ass teeth and his dumb blond surfer-boy haircut. How old is he anyway? What, did he go to vet school when he was twelve?

Really Ace shouldn't be lingering. But he didn't want to leave Ivy and Luke alone. Not when he was looking at her like she was his next meal. Which was why Ace had been in the stables for the past hour, pretending to organize the tack room while secretly watching them do their checks.

"I'll get these samples sent off today, Ivy. Maybe you could come by the practice later in the week to get the results?"

Stop by the practice my ass.

"Sounds good," Ivy beamed. "You think they'll be back by Friday?"

"I don't see why not. Hey, if you come by around closing I might even be able to buy you that drink I owe you?"

"Drinks on you, huh?" Ace could only smirk when Luke's head whipped around to face him, "Hell, I'm in."

Ace knew jealousy didn't look good on him, but this little punk needed to learn some respect. There was no way in hell that Luke hadn't heard the rumors of their engagement.

Yet he continued to flirt with Ivy.

Never one to let a teaching opportunity slide, Ace sauntered over to Ivy and placed his arm around her shoulder. Taking it one step further, he dropped a kiss to her forehead. He ignored the familiar spike in his heart rate that touching her triggered. He was getting good at it. Denial was easy. But, damn, she smelt good. And that, he couldn't ignore. Like jasmine and honey and a fresh summer's day.

"Um … yeah, sounds good." Turns out Luke's smile wasn't always a million dollar one. "Anyway, I best be off."

"Sure." Ivy shot Ace a look before pulling away. "I'll walk you back to your car."

She was pissed. Well, tough. They weren't going to pull this off if the town vet was taking her out on dates. Or trying to.

Maybe I should get her a ring?

That was a good idea. It would go a long way to convincing people and had the added bonus of scaring away any men who dared look in her direction.

He made his way over to Justice's stall. He was Moonrock's money maker. Hopefully. After a few strokes of his chocolate mane, he let the broody thoroughbred sniff his hand.

"You think I should get her a ring, don't you, boy?" Ace chuckled at Justice's snort and gave him a scratch.

"What was that?" Ivy sassed from behind him. He kind of liked this new feisty side of hers that had come out over the course of the week. She'd obviously been hiding it.

"What was what?" He continued to pet Justice.

"You're being an asshole. A weird, jealous asshole. Luke's a nice guy, okay? Jesus, he doesn't even charge me for all the stuff he does around here."

That had Ace turning. "No shit? Well, that'll be 'cause *nice guy Luke* wants in your panties, darlin'."

She was blushing again, and like the dirty bastard Ace was, it only made him think of just how far down that sweet pink flush went.

Now is not the time to be a pervert.

"Don't be ridiculous. He's … he's just being friendly."

He took a step closer to her, and then another and another. Until her intoxicating scent was filling up his lungs. The closer he got, the wider those eyes of hers became.

"Oh, he's being friendly all right. But not for the reasons you're thinking."

Her breathing hitched and he found himself unable to stop himself from reaching out to her. He knew he was playing a dangerous game. But his body and his brain were clearly not on the same page. Using his thumb, he traced her perfect full lips and let the warmth of her breath sink into his skin. "He wants in those pretty little panties of yours. But that's not gonna happen. Wanna know why?" Ace inched closer, until not even air could get between them. "'Cause, sugar … you're mine."

Great, now I'm a possessive pervert.

He kept his eyes on her as she stared up at him. Neither of them spoke, there was only the sound of their ragged breaths filling the barn. It would be so easy to kiss her right now. Replace his thumb with his lips. Make her his. But he couldn't.

"I … uh …" She visibly swallowed and took a step back. She looked flustered. Ruffled. "I need to get Blaze saddled. He … uh … he needs his exercise."

Ace let his hand drop and watched her scurry away. It was for the best. He knew it. So why did he want to chase after her so badly?

***

One of the good things about living with Ivy, that sort of made up for the blue balls, was getting to know her better. He had been right about her hiding parts of herself. As much as he liked the timid, sweet wallflower façade he was initially introduced to, he couldn't deny he preferred the real Ivy much better. The tough, growly, funny, curses-a-lot-more-than-he-thought version.

"Don't tell my mama, but this may be the best chicken pot pie I've ever eaten." Ace shoveled another large piece onto his fork.

Ivy offered him up a small smile as she thanked him.

"Where'd ya learn to cook like this?"

"Oh, um, my nana. But don't go getting any ideas about me being an amazing cook. This is just one out of a few dishes I can actually make without poisoning people." Her lips curved up slightly as her eyes glittered. "Some of my best memories are right here though. In this kitchen. With my nana."

Ace looked around at the dilapidated room they were sitting in. Everything could use updating, from the chipped pine cabinets to the scuffed counters. In fact, the whole house looked like the '80s had vomited on it.

She caught his gaze as his eyes returned to her. "Is that why you kept the place like it is? Preserving the memories. 'Cause I gotta tell you, I'm not sure your nana would like you living like this."

To his surprise Ivy didn't even look a little offended. Which was definitely a good thing. Sometimes he was too honest for his own good.

"Wow." Humor twinkled in her eyes. "Say it like it is, huh? You know you have no filter, right?"

He simply shrugged. "I'm used to saying what's on my mind, I guess. No point beating around the bush and all that. Does it bother you?"

She pondered his question for a moment, her thoughtful gaze lingering on him a little too long. "Not really. It's actually kind of refreshing. I don't know if you've noticed, but I find it kinda hard to lie too."

Oh, he'd noticed all right.

He ignored the new twinge in his chest as her lips curved back into a smile. "Pleased to hear it." After taking another quick glance around the room, he turned his attention back to her. "You know, while I'm here—if you'll let me—I'd be happy to do some work on the house."

"And why would you want to do that? Is that pesky hero complex rearing its ugly head again?"

Ace let out a snigger. It was damn laughable she could even consider him some kind of hero. He was anything but. "Maybe I'm just a nice guy. Ever considered that?"

"Or a sucker for punishment?" She raised a brow.

"Or I have ulterior motives?"

This time, Ivy playfully wiggled her eyebrows. "Oh, really? You after my chicken pot pie recipe?"

"I'm after something." He smirked, feeling slightly gratified by another blush forming. "Oh, I forgot, I've got something for you. Just one sec."

Pushing against the table, he stood and started toward the stairs. Taking two at a time, he was soon in his room and rummaging through the chest of drawers beside his bed.

"Gotcha," he muttered under his breath as he pocketed the box.

Why am I suddenly nervous? It's not real. Get a grip.

Ivy's eyes were all over him as he made his way back into the kitchen.

Is it hot in here?

"Um ..." He was nervous. He was never nervous. How was this even possible? He'd spent his whole life facing down death without breaking a sweat. Now here he was, in this godawful kitchen, with this tiny woman, who was making him perspire to damn near dehydration.

Clearing his throat, he pushed his thoughts aside. "Yeah. So, I was in town earlier and I figured that you would probably need this." Ace dug into the front pocket of his jeans and pulled out the small velvet box. He studied Ivy intently as he carefully placed it on the table in front of her.

Her face was almost comical. Wide cartoon eyes and a jaw that literally hung open. "Ace ... I, uh ... shit."

Maybe it was the stuttering. Maybe it was how vulnerable she looked right then, but something inside of him shifted, and he no longer felt nervous. Hell, he wasn't going to psychoanalyze the what or the why. He wouldn't dare. He was just going to be grateful that he was no longer in danger of leaving a puddle of sweat all over the tiled kitchen floor.

As she flicked open the box and got her first look at the ring, the stuttering continued. "I-I-I uh, oh my God Ace … shit. You didn't have to … I-I mean, I can't accept this. This is … this is …"

He'd already pulled up a chair beside her before she trailed off. For some dumb reason he placed his hand on her arm to comfort her. That's what normal people do, right? Sure they do. He was being normal, damn it. What wasn't freaking normal, though, was the jolt of electricity shooting up his poor, unsuspecting arm as soon as he touched her. No. That wasn't normal at all.

"Sugar, you need a ring if we're gonna convince people we're engaged."

"I know, but this … this is too much." She was still staring in awe at the ring, completely unaware of the sparks now coursing through his veins.

Ace followed her line of sight. The fluorescent bar of light above them had caught the diamonds scattered along the white gold band, making them sparkle even brighter. He had to admit, he might have gone a little overboard when choosing the ring. But when he'd spotted that lush green emerald, the exact color of her eyes, he hadn't been able to stop himself.

"Really, it's no big deal. You needed a ring, so I got you one." As he said it, a thought occurred to him, and the nerves were back. "Don't you like it? I mean, I can exchange it for something else if it's not really your style."

Ivy's eyes snapped back to him. "No, I like it." She twisted in the chair until her whole body was facing him. "I like it a lot, Ace. I'm actually kind of shocked that you could … you picked something so … I love it. That's what I'm trying to say. I love it."

He let out a breath he hadn't been aware he was holding. "Well, good. It's yours. Maybe you could wear it tomorrow

40

night when we go over to Jake and Lily's?"

She slipped the ring onto her finger, and he couldn't look away. "It fits. How did you … was that just a guess?"

He let out a short laugh. There wasn't much humor to it. He just didn't want to look like the creep he was. "Funny story. You had a couple of rings on your dresser." *Or inside your jewelery box, on the shelf, next to your hair ties.* "And I may have, sort of, borrowed them and taken them into town with me."

He waited for her to call him out, but she didn't. She simply studied him, biting down on her bottom lip as she did. What he wouldn't give to know what was going on in that pretty little head of hers.

"I'm gonna go get cleaned up." She rose abruptly, her eyes now adverted. She was concentrating real hard on not looking directly at him. "Leave the dishes, I'll clean everything up later."

He watched her walk away. Wondering what the hell just happened.

***

Ace was not okay. Nothing about tonight was going well. He blamed Ivy. When he'd first gotten a look at her outfit, he'd almost swallowed his tongue. It had made him off balance. Made his desire to loiter in denial a little longer that much harder. And an hour later, he was still off balance.

They were at Jake and Lily's ranch, attending their weekly barbecue. He didn't know Jake all that well, but Brady did, and any friend of Brady's was a friend of his. Not that he was being all that friendly at the moment. His eyes and attention hadn't left Ivy, who was currently huddled around the fire with Brady's wife, Alice.

"Earth to Ace." Brady's hand waved in front of Ace's face, obstructing his view.

"What?" He impatiently pushed his friend's hand away.

"You've been staring at your woman so long, I was

about to grab a drool bucket."

His woman. I like that. If only it were true.

"Fuck off, Mitchell. Like you can keep your eyes off Ali."

Jake simply laughed at them both before excusing himself. Clearly not wanting to be the next one to be dug out. He'd been making moony eyes at his wife, Lily, and baby daughter ever since Ace had arrived.

"What the hell is up with you tonight, man?"

Ace snatched another look at Ivy before returning his gaze back to Brady. "She's wearing that goddamn dress. I don't know, man." He shoved his fingers through his shaggy hair, no doubt messing it up even more. "It's not that she doesn't look good in jeans and a tank, but fucking hell. She's killing me. Do you see what she's wearing? Tell me it's not frigging distracting?"

He needed some validity. Some acknowledgment. That she did look damn near breathtaking, and he wasn't losing his ever-loving mind.

"I think I'm the wrong man to ask, buddy. Ali's got me whipped to fuck." He chuckled. The smug bastard.

"Yeah, never mind. Ignore me. I'm just losing it, man."

"Come on, brother." Brady clapped him on the back. "We both know what's going on here. You're falling for her. I don't see what the problem is."

"Yeah. You wouldn't."

"Now you're the fucking Riddler? You gonna tell me what that means?"

Ace took another swig of his beer. The cold shot combined with the cooler fall air managed to awaken his senses and clear his head a little. "Don't be a dumbass. I'll give you a clue. Take a look at my face."

"You're telling me this is about your burns? Jesus Christ." Brady shook his head, before letting out a heavy sigh. "You think that Ivy gives two shits about your scars? You're fucking blind, man. I've seen the way that girl looks at you. And I'm telling you now, man, she doesn't care."

It was easy for his friend to just brush him off. He wasn't

the one living with these scars. Ace was the one who got stared at. He was the one who scared little kids. He was the one that faced down hushed whispers everywhere he went. It was the kind of attention that made him move to Bluestone in the first place.

Have a pity party, why don't you?

"It's not just that. I mean, it is and it's not. It's like you said when you warned me off her. I'm not exactly a relationship kinda guy. And even if I was, I'm hardly in a position to offer much to any woman, especially since … well, y'know, since I'm dealing with all this"—he used his good arm to point at his torso—"new face, fucked up arm, missing skin across half my goddamn chest. Come on, man. I'm hardly a fucking catch and you know it."

Brady's dark eyes narrowed on Ace. Brady was assessing. He did that a lot now. Maybe it was a cop thing. Whatever he was about to say, he didn't get a chance to, though, as they were joined by Ivy and Alice.

Good. Ace knew he wouldn't have wanted to hear what his friend had to say anyway.

Conveniently, Ace hadn't gotten around to telling Ivy that his friend knew their relationship was fake and likely his wife did too. And right then, he felt guilty and unsure of what to do. Was he supposed to play along with the fake fiancé thing when everyone present knew it was bullshit? Or maybe it didn't matter, because there were other people in the vicinity that they could put on a show for?

Before he could come to a definitive decision, Ivy wrapped her arm around his waist and leaned against him. *Shit.* He hadn't expected that. Immediately, he tensed up. Everywhere.

"You have to see Ivy's ring, baby; it's so fucking beautiful," Alice practically screeched, bringing Ace out of his near-frozen state.

Ivy quickly untangled herself, and he instantly missed her. He could swear she left scorch marks. She proudly placed her left hand in front of Brady, a luminous smile lighting up her delicate features.

Brady let out a low whistle. "Holy shit." Ace knew what was coming, his friend was grinning from ear to ear. "That must have set you back a pretty penny, brother?"

He shot his friend a look, but didn't answer. Brady would have to bag on Ace later. He didn't stay pissed for too long, though, because the next thing he knew, Ivy's body was pressed against him again, her arm reaching around and pulling him closer.

"I'm one lucky girl, that's for sure."

How the hell was he supposed to not fall for this woman?

CHAPTER FIVE

Ivy had made a decision. She was no longer going to allow Ace to affect her. Yes. Decision made. She was done. A week into living together and despite her beginning to feel more comfortable around him, from this day forward, he was officially forbidden. The forbidden fruit as it were. And she had no intention of feasting on his forbidden fruit. No frigging way.

It was clear now that throwing herself at Ace, no matter how tempting, was possibly the worst idea in the history of very bad ideas. Yes, he was hot, but their situation was beyond complicated. He was her live-in fake fiancé for God's sake. And she needed to keep reminding herself of that and exactly why he was there in the first place. Her business. The most important thing in her life.

She also wouldn't let herself forget the man's mood swings. If anything did ever happen between them, there was no way she wouldn't come out the other end not burned to a crisp. Either from the fire he continually seemed to ignite in her or from the damn freezer burns he left behind when he flipped from hot to cold.

Last night had been a lot. The way Ace's eyes had followed her around all night had been intense. And confusing. But in classic Ace fashion, once they had arrived back at Moonrock, it had been as if someone had lit a fire up his ass. He was up the stairs and behind his bedroom door before she had a chance to blink.

So today, she was going out. All day. She needed a day off the ranch and away from Ace to clear her head. All she had to do was get out of the house unscathed. And apparently that was easier said than done.

"Morning," she squeaked as she abruptly came to a halt in the hallway, narrowly escaping bumping into Ace as he exited the bathroom.

Of course the man was half naked. Dripping wet, in just a towel. Damnit. Why did God hate her? Was she being punished for something? This wasn't fair. There was fruit just flying all over the place. Her traitorous eyes darted straight to the V-shaped muscle above the white cotton. It was taunting her. An arrow. Pointing to everything that she definitely wasn't thinking about.

Deep breaths, Ivy. Control yourself. At least pretend you have some dignity.

Her gaze wandered back up to a more appropriate body part, his face. Perfectly chiseled, with drops of water clinging to his dark, day-old stubble.

"You never look." Ace's deep voice was rougher than she was used to.

"What?"

"At my burns. You never look at them. Why is that?"

It's not like she didn't realize he had scars. She wasn't an idiot. But they weren't all that important to her. They were just there. Just another part of him. They didn't detract from how hot the man was, that was for sure. Maybe she'd see them differently if she'd known him before. But she hadn't.

"I don't know. I've never really thought about it. Why?"

She felt like this was some sort of test. But it was too early, and he was way too naked for her to pass.

"I guess you're the first person I've met—since it happened—who doesn't flinch or stare. Even now, with the full extent of my very fucked-up body on display, it's like you haven't even noticed. I don't get it."

Ivy wanted to comfort him. Go to him. Run her hands over the puckered skin and convince him how perfect he was, not stop until he saw what she does.

No. No. No. Control yourself, woman. Forbidden fricking fruit, damnit.

"Your body isn't fucked up, Ace." Warily, she took a step toward him, but kept a healthy distance. "It's just different now, from what you were used to. I guess to me, I've only known this version. And maybe there are just other places on you I'd rather be looking at."

Did I just say that? Shit.

If the glint in Ace's eyes were anything to go by, he wasn't going to let that comment slide. She felt herself gulp as he stalked toward her and quickly closed the distance between them.

"Oh yeah, and where would you rather be looking, sugar?"

Her brain was too fuzzy for this. It was filled with his freshly showered scent. Sandalwood, menthol and something citrusy she couldn't quite put her finger on.

"I just … I just meant that, uh … that the burns don't define you. How you look and stuff. You're still a good-looking guy."

Was that better or worse? Damn scent scrambling her brain cells.

Blue flames danced in his eyes as she felt the heat of his minty breath sink into her skin. *Oh no.* "You think I'm good-looking, huh?"

"Sure. You're all right." Nonchalant was much harder to pull off when you're blushing. So, she wasn't that surprised by the smug smirk he flashed her.

"Just all right?"

"I don't want you to get a big head."

"Heaven forbid."

"I, um. I'm heading out for the day. So, I … I better get

going." Her head was telling her to run, but her stupid body wasn't cooperating. It had been doing that a lot lately.

Ace was in no rush to move either. In fact, it felt like he'd managed to get even closer. When did that happen? The slight dip of his head put his mouth just inches away from hers.

Goddamnit.

"What's the rush, sugar?"

She was drowning in those deep pools. It was a problem. She couldn't move. He was holding her in place with them.

Right now, his proximity was hindering any chance of her being able to string a complete sentence together. So, she didn't reply. But the silence didn't help the situation. If anything, it made it worse. Their combined heavy breaths filtering through her ears felt like some sort of aphrodisiac.

When his lips brushed against hers, it was over. All rational thought flew out the window. He took his time tasting her. Teasing her. And she let him. His lips were soft, gentle, and exploratory. But there was nothing sweet about this kiss. It was a promise of what was to come. Of the time he was going to take pleasing her. And as soon as she opened for him, his tongue was inside of her, deepening the kiss until she was physically aching for him.

His big hands took hold of her hips and pulled her flush against him. Every part of him was hard. The man was pure muscle, and her treacherous body was loving every second. Wrapping her hands around his neck, she gave into the tingles and angled her face so she could take him deeper.

As he maneuvered her against the wall, she knew they were heading into dangerous territory. Especially when his hands started to move up the length of her vest and only stopped when his thumbs were brushing the underside of her breasts. God, he felt good.

Pulling back slightly, he nipped her lower lip, immediately making her gasp. Moments later, his tongue was taking care of the sting, before his lips were on the move again, making their way along her jawline until they reached her earlobe.

"You're so fucking sexy." His voice was ragged, thick with lust.

Everything was hazy; she could barely hear him over the sound of her heartbeat. How was it possible to lose your mind over a kiss? This had never happened to her before. She felt drunk. Drunk on him. Drunk on his taste, his smell, his touch. And just when she thought it couldn't get any better, his lips latched onto the curve of her neck.

"Jesus fucking Christ," slipped from her lips as her head arched back.

The man was pure sin. She wanted him. She'd never wanted a man so much in all her life. It was her turn to touch. Dropping her hands from his shoulders, she slid them over his torso, beginning her journey just above the towel. Her fingers were sliding over every ridge and ripple. When she reached the mottled skin that made up most of his left side though, he froze. The air stilled. She knew in that moment, that was it. He was going to run. And she was right.

"I can't." A second later, his lips were no longer on her, and he had gone to the trouble of taking a large step back. "I'm sorry, I can't."

And then he was gone.

***

So, she'd lasted what, a good ten minutes? Possibly twelve minutes? Between making the decision to stay the hell away from Ace and then sticking her tongue down his throat.

Excellent. Good work, Ivy. Ever the overachiever.

At least she'd gotten away from the ranch. Not unscathed like she'd intended. She was definitely scathed.

Acutely aware she was greatly lacking in the friend's department, she'd found herself at Mickey's. She'd gone crawling straight to her brother.

"Tell me again why you're here on a Saturday? Don't you have chores to do?" Teddy continued to stack glasses behind the bar.

Sadly, she was aware of just how early it was. Way too early to have already endured a traumatic event. She was just glad her brother had been here when she'd decided to start banging down the door.

Ivy twiddled with the straw in her Coke. "I just wanted to see my big brother. That's all. Nothing sketchy."

Wait. Does saying it's not sketchy make it seem more sketchy?

Teddy snorted and disappeared below the bar for a moment. When he reappeared, it was to place a large box of wine onto the counter. "Bullshit doesn't suit you, sis. You have a fight with the marine?"

This was about the time she wished she had a girlfriend to confide in. There was Alice. But Ivy feared that Alice may be a little too close to the whole situation, being Ace's best friend's wife and all. She really should have made more of an effort to make friends when her ones from high school left town. But she'd always been so busy. Taking care of her grandparents. Taking care of the ranch. It never left her much time for herself, let alone a social life.

"If I say yes, are you gonna go down there and kick his ass?" It was always a strong possibility.

Teddy's thick eyebrow arched. "Depends. Do you want me to go down there and kick his ass?"

"No. I just need to make sure you don't go all alpha male on me if I talk to you about my love life."

Her brother pushed the box away and settled his elbows on the bar. "Ivy, you can tell me anything. I promise. But I'm telling you right now, if that motherfucker hurts you, I'll hurt him. You're my little sister. I can't help it if I'm protective of you."

"I'm thirty."

"So?"

It was like banging her head against a brick wall. "Can't you just not be my brother for one minute and be my friend?"

The creases in his brow unwrinkled. "What happened?" There was that easy, gentler tone he usually reserved for his customers.

"Nothing really." She was lying, but just because she wasn't ready to come clean didn't mean she didn't want his advice. "I think ... I think what happened to him is screwing with him, and I'm worried about him."

"Ivy, come on. The man's got burns covering half his body, of course it's screwing with him. You don't think something like that would screw with you?"

"Yeah, of course. It's just I don't know what to do to help him deal, y'know? The way he talks about himself. He sees himself as this damaged thing, and I don't know what to do to help him see what I see."

Everything she was saying was true. As much as it hurt to have Ace walk away from her. She got why. He hadn't accepted his scars yet, so he couldn't understand why someone else would. Why she wanted to touch him. Why she wanted him. But now she was stuck between a rock and a hard place because she had no idea where to go from here.

"Look, he's not gonna get over something like that overnight. And being with you, letting you in, that must have been a big step for him. A step in the right direction, I reckon. Trust me, sis, letting you love him, all of him, is going to do more good than you know."

That was the problem though. He wasn't with her. He hadn't let her in. But in a strange sort of way, she could see how that would probably help. Maybe that was the answer after all. She had to show him how perfect he was, just as he is. She needed to seduce him.

Sure, it's for his own good. This is no way related to you wanting in his pants.

Pushing aside the unhelpful commentary, she rose from her barstool. She had shopping to do. And a man to seduce.

CHAPTER SIX

Ace was on his way back to Moonrock. Spending the night at Brady's might have been slightly dramatic, but he'd needed the distance, if only for a night. He needed to regroup and get his head on straight. Because like a dumbass, he'd kissed Ivy. And then swiftly hightailed it out of there without so much of an explanation.

She hadn't called him though. Not even when she must have come home to an empty house last night. He supposed it was likely because she was pissed. Or worse, upset. The last thing he wanted to do was hurt her. But that's exactly what he would've done if he had let that kiss go any further.

As he started down the gravel road to the ranch, his anxiety kicked up a notch. He didn't know how to play this. Seeing Ivy again was going to be difficult. Now he'd kissed her, now it was no longer a fantasy but a reality, it was going to be the ultimate test of his restraint.

He wanted her. So much. That had been the best damned kiss of his life. But the second her perfect, soft skin had touched his corrupted flesh, he was reminded of just why he couldn't have her. He was a freak. A shell of a man. She deserved more. Better. She deserved everything.

That was why he was going back. He was a man of his

word. And if helping her with the ranch was all he could ever offer her, then he would throw all his energy into making it a success. Today they had a meeting with a potential new client. A meeting Ivy would be attending. So, there was no hiding from her.

Once he'd parked outside the main house, he went inside and did a quick scan for Ivy. She wasn't there. After that, he made his way down to the office. A small cabin across from the stables. If she wasn't in the house, she was normally there. He didn't bother knocking, but he was soon regretting that.

What. The. Fuck.

She was wearing daisy freaking dukes and bending over a pile of folders next to her desk. He was going to have a heart attack. This was it. This was how he was going to die. She was going to kill him. Why the hell was she wearing tiny ass shorts in the middle of fall? Actually, an even better question was why was she dressed like this when they were about to meet with a new client? *Is that?* Sweet Jesus, the shorts had ridden up. He bit down on his now very clenched fist.

Dear Lord, give me strength.

Her wearing this, bending like that, it felt like a trap. A trap he very much wanted to be caught in. This was definitely a new kind of torture. The fact that he wasn't across the room, spinning her around and helping himself to another taste was a damn miracle. He deserved a medal.

"Ivy." He was hanging on to the last of his control by a thread, so he knew his tone was clipped and impatient. "Evan will be here any minute. Maybe you should go change?"

Ivy snapped up and whipped around, her long wavy brown hair almost slapping her in the face with the force of her sudden movements. "I'm surprised you even bothered to turn up."

Oh, yeah, she's pissed all right.

She placed her dainty hands on her hips and took her

time looking him up and down. He used that time to not stare at how long and silky her bare legs looked. And he definitely didn't notice how tight her tank top was or how it clung to each and every curve.

"And no, I don't plan on changing."

There was no way in hell he was going to let Evan get an eyeful of Ivy. Not in this obscene outfit. Well, obscene was a slight exaggeration, but it didn't exactly leave much to the imagination. And as far as Ace was concerned, this sight before him should be reserved for his eyes only.

"You think it's appropriate to meet a potential client in short shorts?"

"I don't know if you noticed, asshole, but it's a hundred fricking degrees in here. The heat is broken, and I can't shut it off. So, under the circumstances, yes, shorts are preferable to Evan shaking hands with a big puddle of sweat."

Asshole? That's new. Shit. Why am I so turned on by her calling me out? Jesus, I am an asshole. A sick one.

All right, so it was a bit balmy in there. It was safe to say his attention had not been on the temperature of the room when he'd walked in. And the heat currently pumping through his veins had been caused by something else entirely.

"Ivy. I'm serious. Put on some fucking jeans."

She smirked. A devilish glint in her eyes as she slowly approached him. "What's a matter, Ace? My bare legs offending you?" Her glittering eyes never left his as she closed the distance between them. "Scared of a little skin, huh? Why is that?" She tilted her head and gave him a sultry smile. "Afraid you won't be able to control yourself?"

Damnit. It was a trap. She knew exactly what she was doing. And it was working. He practically growled as the familiar waft of jasmine and honey filled his lungs. "You're playing with fire, sugar."

"Oh, yeah? You wanna stop, drop, and roll with me?"

He bit back a laugh. This was not funny. She was not funny.

Luckily, he was saved by a hard knock on the door. Evan had arrived.

***

Turns out Evan wasn't just interested in Justice, he'd also taken a shine to Blaze and Zeus, one of their younger studs.

Maybe it was because Evan was nearer their age, but he didn't seem to have an issue dealing with Ivy. It was obvious throughout the meeting she was the one running the show. And he had no problem going over the details with her and directing all his questions her way. She was in her element, and Ace couldn't have been prouder.

Although on occasion, he did have to keep a handle on his jealousy. She was still wearing those goddamn shorts and from the way Evan had been side-glancing Ivy the whole time, it was obvious he'd noticed too. Doing business with an unmarried woman clearly wasn't an issue for Evan. If anything, Ace suspected it was preferable.

"That went way better than I expected," Ivy announced as they watched Evan's truck disappear beyond the horizon.

"He was impressed, Ivy. You impressed him. You really were amazing back there."

After biting down on her lower lip, her gaze zeroed in on her boots. It was clear the woman wasn't used to compliments. Which was absurd. She deserved to be showered in compliments every second of every day.

"Don't."

"Don't what? Tell the truth?"

"I don't need your flattery or your pity, Ace."

Before he could reply, she'd started heading toward the house. He quickly followed after her, suppressing a groan as he caught sight of the sexy sway of her ass in those evil denim shorts.

As soon as she reached the front door, his hand was over her shoulder and pushing down on the wood, preventing her entry.

"First of all, that wasn't flattery, it was an observation. You're good at what you do, Ivy. You know your shit. And you're a damn fine businesswoman, despite what that asshole Donoghue would have everyone believe. Secondly, and more importantly, trust me when I say, the last thing I feel for you is pity."

Ivy twisted to face Ace, and he mentally cursed himself for allowing himself to be this close to her again. "And what is it you feel for me, Ace?"

The way she was looking at him now wasn't full of the same playful sass and grit he'd witnessed earlier. It had an air of unease and vulnerability, yet it still managed to fill him with the same want he felt earlier. The same want that made his stomach tight and his palms sweat. She was a plethora of contradictions. A mixture of sweet and shy with a healthy dose of stubbornness and fire thrown in for good measure. And he loved it all. She was perfect. Unique. Special.

Goddamnit.

What he wouldn't give to pull her close and kiss away the uncertainty clouding those beautiful green eyes. But no. He couldn't. Not now. Not ever. She wasn't his. And he had to keep reminding himself of that.

"Inside, Ivy." He pulled his hand away from the door and took a step back. "I'll make us coffee before we make a start on the paperwork."

A flash of disappointment crossed her face before she schooled it. That wasn't what she wanted to hear. Too bad. Deflecting and avoidance were all he had right now.

"You gonna tell me where you were last night?"

He followed her into the kitchen and made a beeline for the coffeepot. "Brady's."

"Oh. Did you tell them we had an argument or something?"

Right. He hadn't told her.

"No. I didn't need to." He slowly turned and rested his behind against the kitchen counter. "Actually, Ivy, I should have told you sooner … but Brady knows."

"Knows what?" Her eyes widened in panic. He wasn't handling this very well.

"About the whole fake fiancé thing," Ace confirmed. "And as he doesn't keep secrets from his wife, Alice knows too."

That panic he saw turned quickly to anger. It was time to turn around again and focus on the coffee.

"Are you being fucking serious?"

"Brady's like a brother; I can't lie to him. Plus, he kinda guessed."

Small hands were pushing at his bicep, forcing him to turn and face a very angry-looking Ivy. She looked like steam might come out of her ears any second. It was kind of cute. But he was keeping that thought to himself.

"I lied to my *actual* brother, you asshole."

That was the second time today she'd called him an asshole, and he had a feeling he'd hear it again before the day was up. "

"You gonna tell me why you didn't tell me this … oh, I don't know … a week ago! God, I must have looked like such an idiot at that barbecue, pretending we were together when everyone knew."

He took hold of her shoulders and stared into her. "Everyone didn't know, Ivy. I swear. Only Brady and Alice. Lily and Jake don't know, nor do anyone else who was there. You didn't look like an idiot at all. If anything, I did. I was all over you, remember? In front of Brady, in front of Alice. Even when I knew they knew."

That didn't come out the way he thought it would. Why had he said that? Talk about a slip.

"Why did you?"

He should have known Ivy wasn't going to let him off the hook that easily.

"I don't know." *Liar.* "I guess I got carried away." *Coward.*

Letting his hands drop, he went back to the coffee and surrendered to the internal beating he was about to give himself.

***

Ivy had lost her damn mind. And in turn, was making Ace lose his too. If he didn't know any better, he would think the woman was up to something.

It hadn't registered until this very minute. Sure, the daisy dukes she'd greeted him in three days ago were a little out of character, but the heat in the office had genuinely been broken. Running into her in just a towel also wasn't all that suspicious, seeing as they shared a bathroom. But this morning she'd come down to the kitchen in the tiniest nightie he'd ever seen. And right this second, she was officially topless. In the barn.

What the hell?

He was gawking. Like a teenage boy. She had a bra on. It shouldn't be a big deal. But it was. Because it was Ivy in a bra. A sexy blue, lacy bra, that revealed a chest, which was much larger and more perfect than even his imagination had conjured up.

"Sorry." She must have noticed his expression if the slight smirk was anything to go by. "That was a lot of drool. I think I'm gonna ask Luke to come by and check him out, make sure he hasn't got an infection."

Drool or no drool, she didn't have to rip off her damn shirt.

She better put a top on before that motherfucker Luke gets here. Or better yet, a big ass coat.

Ace's jaw involuntarily clenched at the thought of Luke seeing her like this.

How had this happened? It had only been three days since he'd sworn to keep things professional, and he was already struggling. Well, if he was being honest, he'd been breaking a sweat ever since he saw her in those short shorts. But now this. Now, she was topless, and his body was pretty much rebelling and all logical thought had fled.

He was about a millisecond away from grabbing her and taking what he wanted. But then she left. Walked out of the barn, most likely to go and find another shirt. He should be happy. Relieved even. But he wasn't. And now he didn't know what to do.

CHAPTER SEVEN

Ivy was starting to question herself. Maybe Ace really wasn't interested in her and it was all in her head. She'd practically engaged in a three-day strip show and the man hadn't so much as blinked.

She looked back at herself in the mirror and bit down on her lip. There was no point changing her mind now. Even if Ace didn't respond to her outfit, she could still go out and have a good time with Alice, maybe Ivy would even attract a new man.

I don't want a new man. I want Ace.

That thought was sobering. She couldn't remember a time when she wanted a man so much. She couldn't decide if that was a testament to how much she liked Ace or how incredibly sad her life was.

Ivy smoothed down the fabric on the black dress. This wasn't exactly her usual style; she'd bought it on a whim. Well, not a whim so much as a seduction mission. It was short and tight. It screamed *look at me*. And she wasn't really that sure she wanted anyone looking at her except Ace.

No matter what, she was going out. She'd arranged the girls' night with Alice, not only so she could wear this dress, but so she could talk to someone other than Ace, who knew about their charade. There was no doubt she was in desperate need of advice.

Taking a deep breath, she checked her reflection one more time before exiting her bedroom. As she made it down the creaky stairs, she could hear the television blasting. There must be a game on. At least she didn't have to hunt him down to show off her outfit.

Thankfully her keys were on the coffee table, so she had an excuse to see him. She didn't miss the whip of his head as she entered, or the way his eyes bugged out as he caught sight of what she was wearing.

Fucking finally. Some sort of reaction.

Putting on her most nonchalant face, she went straight for her keys, still feeling the heat of his stare drag over her.

"Um, Ivy … two questions. Where are you going? And what the hell are you wearing?" Although Ace may have thought his tone was calm, the raise in his voice during the last question gave him away.

"Mickey's. I'm meeting Ali for drinks." She offered him a bright smile before sashaying toward the front door. "Don't wait up!"

She didn't make it that far. A strong arm reached out, spun her, and a big body backed her against the wall. Ace's big body, crowding her, both of his hands were on the wall on either side of her face.

"You wanna explain to me why my fiancée is about to leave the house in a dress designed to bring grown men to their knees?"

That was a slight exaggeration. "Fake fiancée," she corrected, "and I'm not sure I know what you mean."

"Don't play dumb, sugar. You know exactly what I mean." His breathing was getting shallow, and his voice had changed. It was huskier than usual. Rougher. And it managed to send tingles down her spine. "You wore that dress for a reason. You care to share that reason?"

"You seem to have it all figured out." Damnit. Now her voice was all breathy.

Ace tilted his head until their faces were aligned, and his darkened eyes were holding her in place. He was so close she couldn't think. Even the smell of his cologne was making her a little lightheaded.

"I think you're trying to get my attention."

"And why would I want to do that?"

"So I'll do this …"

His mouth crashed down on her hard. It wasn't at all like their first kiss. This one seemed almost angry. His tongue, easily prying her lips apart, took possession of her instantly. And she couldn't help but moan into his mouth as he took the kiss deeper and deeper.

One of his hands cupped her face, moving her into a position that allowed him more control. The other hand came to her waist and lightly tugged until her body was pressed firmly against his.

Pulling his tongue back, he kept his lips on her. "This what you want, sugar?" Teasing her, his teeth scraped across her lower lip. "Say it." His demand was fiercer this time. The boom of his voice vibrating down her throat.

She managed a somewhat breathless *yes*, which seemed to satisfy him, as seconds later he was prising her mouth apart again.

They swallowed each other's groans as he continued to consume her. To say the dress had worked was an understatement. It had turned Ace positively feral.

She didn't get to enjoy it for long though. The sound of her phone ringing managed to awake at least a couple of her lust-riddled brain cells. But as she attempted to pull away, Ace kept her lips hostage. "I have to … I have to get that," she mumbled against his lips.

He simply growled and went back for another taste. The phone stopped ringing but pinged with a message. It was undoubtedly Alice, probably wondering where the hell she was. That thought had Ivy's brain turning back on, and she managed to pull free this time.

"Ali is waiting for me, Ace. I need to go." Ivy reluctantly

pushed on his rock-hard chest and let out a sigh.

Her gaze braved his and his face was as raw with need as he'd felt. "I'm driving you there, and I'm picking you up. Any man comes near you tonight, you show them that ring of yours, you hear me?"

Jesus Christ. Why does the whole jealousy thing look so damn sexy on him?

Instead of answering, she kissed him again. It was gentler. Softer. And over before she let herself get carried away. She slowly drew back, keeping her eyes on him and running her fingers over his stubble as she did.

"Let's go."

***

"So let me get this straight." Alice downed the rest of her drink before leveling Ivy with her so-called serious face. "You guys are pretending to be together even though you actually are together?"

"We're not together," Ivy insisted. She was doing a terrible job of explaining things. "We kissed ... twice. That is not *together*."

Ivy took another glance around the bar. Thankfully it was Teddy's night off. He would not approve of her dress, and God only knows what kind of scene he might have caused if he'd caught two of his regulars trying to hit on her.

"That sounds pretty damn together to me." Alice's voice pulled Ivy out of her head. "I mean, kissing leads to other things, and other things lead to ... Well, I mean, the next thing you know ... bam! You're in a relationship! Trust me, I know. Also, can we please talk about this gigantic rock on your finger?"

Ivy instinctively lifted her hand and watched as the rocks sparkled despite the dim lighting. It was the most beautiful ring she'd ever seen. If she ever were to get married one day, this would be the ring she would want.

Alice picked up Ivy's hand and poured over the emerald.

"It's one thing to suggest he be your fake fiancé, Ivy. It's something else entirely to go out and buy a damn engagement ring. Not just any engagement ring at that. This one." She shook her hand for emphasis. "This ring was so clearly picked out specifically for you and must have cost a near blooming fortune. Oh, and how the hell did he know your ring size?"

"He took one of my rings to the jewelers." Ivy quietly mumbled but regretted the words as soon as she noticed Alice's face light up.

"He took one of your rings," Alice repeated and shook her head. "Holy fucking shit, girl. The man is gone for you!"

Feeling nervous, Ivy started to fiddle with her straw. It wasn't that she thought Ace was actually "gone for her," it was more the realization that she was in fact gone for him.

Ivy thought back to her journey over to Mickey's tonight. Even though they didn't address the kiss on the ride over, Ace had made it clear he was no longer running.

Fear started to creep in. She knew she was being stupid. This had been what she wanted all along. He was what she wanted, but the reality of it all felt so much scarier. She was out of her comfort zone. Out of her league.

"How the hell do I do this, Ali?" Ivy blurted.

"Do what?"

"Ace, this thing between us, how do I do this? I haven't been on a date in what … like, five years."

Alice choked on her drink at that particular revelation. After wiping her mouth, she tried to mask her shock. She was doing a bad job.

"Five years. Fuck. That's a long arse time, Ivy. I take it that means you've not been laid in that long either?"

"Uh … that'll be a no."

Ivy witnessed a succession of horrified headshakes. Alice was going to make herself dizzy at this rate. "You should go home right now and get on that. I'm serious. You need to climb that man like a tree. That's my advice. Go home, take your clothes off, and sort that shit out."

"Ali!" Ivy pushed at Alice's shoulder. This was not helping. "What the hell! Your advice is to go jump him?"

"Um … yeah. Duh. It's been five frigging years, Ivy. You have a hot man living in your house who you want. Who wants you right back. Stop overthinking things and go get you some."

Could it really be that simple?

CHAPTER EIGHT

They'd just returned from Mickey's and Ivy was still in that tight little dress. The dress that had single-handedly unraveled the last thread of his restraint.

He hadn't been able to stop thinking about her the whole night. And he was sure he could still feel the imprint of her lips against his. It was pathetic. He was pathetic. Like some lovesick puppy.

Now here they were, in the kitchen, pretending as if the electricity currently making the room pulsate wasn't there and definitely wasn't going to cause one or both of them to spontaneously combust at any second.

It may not be the most gentlemanly thing to do, but he couldn't wait any longer. He had to have her. Tonight. Since the very first moment he'd lain eyes on her, she'd haunted his dreams. Now he was ready for the real thing. He needed to touch her. Taste her. Explore every single part of her until they were both boneless.

Decision made, he stalked toward the counter she was leaning against. As soon as he was close enough, he dipped his head until they were a breath apart. Before taking what he wanted, he waited for any indication she wasn't on board. Her breath hitched in anticipation, but she didn't move away. A good sign.

"I want you, Ivy. I don't wanna fight it anymore." He lightly dragged his fingertips over the pretty pink stains highlighting her cheek and felt her tremble beneath his touch. "Say the word and I'll stop."

"I don't want you to stop," she whispered, her hooded eyes holding him captive.

That was all he needed to hear. Catching her rosy lips, she immediately opened for him. As he got his first taste of her, he couldn't stop the guttural groan ripping through him. She was sweeter than sugar. A mixture of Coke, honey, and something so uniquely Ivy. It had the hairs on the back of his neck standing to attention. She was a goddess.

Slipping his hand around to the back of her neck, he held her firmly in place so he could take what he wanted. Taking pleasure in swallowing her whimpers, he let the raw heat wash over him as he pressed into her.

Ivy's dainty fingers slid down his shirt and headed straight toward the hem. As she pushed under, the heat of her touch practically singed his skin. It was inevitable that she would soon reach his scars and he could already feel his muscles start to tense.

Ivy must have sensed his apprehension, as much to his distress, she slowed their kiss. In between ragged breaths, she murmured against his lips, "Take off your shirt."

This was it. He wished it could be different. That he could leave his clothes on. At least the first time, but he already knew Ivy wouldn't stand for it.

Fuck. Why is this so hard?

Pulling back, she aimed her glazed eyes at his. "I want to see you, Ace. I want to touch you. Please."

He found himself swallowing hard at the sight of her. The heavy rise and fall of her chest was mesmerizing, coupled with her wet, swollen lips and flushed cheeks. Perfection. Not able to deny her, he used one hand around the back of his neck to shrug off his shirt and watched her eyes widen. Thankfully not in disgust. No. There was only fire there.

Closing the gap between them, she placed soft kisses around the edges of his mouth. Lightly moving across his puckered skin, her lips grazed his jaw, then his cheekbones, and traveled all the way over to his ear. Taking his earlobe in between her teeth, she gently bit down until goosebumps covered his whole body. When her wicked tongue ran over the teeth marks, he thought he was having an out-of-body experience. This woman was something else.

His heart was thumping at a worrying speed as her lips slid down his throat. No one who wasn't a nurse or a doctor had ever touched his burns. He'd never allowed it. Not even his family got near him. So, to have Ivy's mouth on them was a whole new experience. He had to admit, he didn't hate it.

He let her tongue glide across his chest for probably a minute before he just couldn't take it anymore. Lifting her chin with one hand, the other reached behind her dress and unzipped.

"Off. Now." Even he didn't miss the need lacing his command.

Ivy complied and seductively shimmied out of her dress, revealing a matching black lace underwear set. He was a goner. Any small semblance of control he thought he might have had was tossed out of the window.

Right now, he needed a bed. Lifting her with ease, he gathered her in his arms. Ivy let out a small gasp in shock, but he could tell she'd settled in for the ride as soon as she wrapped her arms around his neck. Once he was sure that she was secure, he wasted no time heading toward the stairs.

"Ace." The uncertainty in her voice had him stopping mid-step. Was she having second thoughts?

When she went quiet, he urged her to continue. "Yeah, darlin'?"

"Will you ... will you be gentle with me?" If he hadn't already stopped, those words would have done it.

He set her down on her feet so he could look into those

emeralds as he spoke. "Sugar, if you're not ready, we don't have to do this. I can wait. We can wait. For as long as you need."

Ivy's hand went straight to his face and cupped his cheek. "No. That's not what I ..." She paused for a moment, obviously trying to find the right words. "I'm ready. It's just that it's been a long time for me. I guess what I'm saying is that I just need you to bear with me. That's all. Is that okay?"

Is that okay? Was she kidding? He would do anything for her. Go any pace she wanted.

"That's more than okay. Hell, it's been a long time for me too. And I haven't, uh"—he cleared his throat—"I haven't been with anyone since, y'know ..."

She nodded in understanding before wrapping her arms around him. "I'm ready to be picked up again."

He chuckled at her cute demand and hauled her back up, tucking her safely against his chest once again. She fit perfectly in his arms. Like she was made just for him.

***

He'd never done this before. How was he supposed to do this? Last night had been incredible. More than incredible. Out of this world. A part of him had always known things would be different with Ivy. She was different. But now it was confirmed, and he had no idea what to do next.

The last time he'd had any sort of a relationship was in high school, and even then he wasn't sure it could be classed as one. It was more making out in between classes than sharing any sort of deep emotional connection. He'd certainly never felt for anyone the way he felt for Ivy.

Ivy squirmed in his hold. Bringing his attention back to the soft woman lying beside him. Her legs were still tangled with his, but her hips were beginning to buck into him. Considering the placement of her very bare ass in his very naked lap, she was playing a dangerous game. There was only so much self-control a man could muster.

"Morning, sugar, you sleep well?"

She let out a sexy mew before playfully bucking her hips again. "I did ... you sure know how to tire a girl out."

Letting out a chuckle, he tightened his hold across her stomach and pulled her closer until the warmth of her soft skin was penetrating his chest.

His mouth hovered over her ear until he could feel her shiver. "Sugar," he rumbled, "you move that pretty little ass one more time and you're gonna get a spanking. I'm holding on by a thread here."

Her stomach vibrated against his hand as she started to giggle. She twisted in his hold until they were face to face but no less close.

"I think you're gonna need to work on your threats." Ivy smirked. "That's not much of a deterrent."

God, she looked so beautiful in the morning. Whispers of sunlight crept through the curtain cracks and lit up her green eyes, which looked a whole shade lighter. The way she was looking at him made his heart constrict. He'd not felt like a man in a long time. She made him feel like one, like the man he used to be. Before.

He wished it was as simple as just sex. That getting laid post-injury had fixed what had been broken inside of him. But it wasn't that. It was Ivy. The connection they shared. The things he felt. It had shifted something inside of him. Dislodged a broken piece that had been preventing him from healing.

Ivy didn't see his scars. She saw the man behind them. He didn't realize until now just how much he needed that. To finally be seen. Wanted. Sure, he'd been wanted plenty in the past. For his looks, for his job, for his money. Not like this though. Nothing compared to this. She wanted him. All of him. Homeless, jobless, scarred to shit. None of that mattered to her.

Screw self-control.

Slamming his lips down onto hers, he used her shocked gasp to his advantage and thrust his tongue into her mouth. She tasted just as sweet as she did last night. One of her hands curled around his bicep, while the other swept over the muscles on his chest. It did nothing to slow down his heart rate or his now overwhelming sense of urgency to have her again.

He tore himself away from her plumped lips so he could get another taste of that creamy skin. Gliding down the nape of her neck, he lightly bit down on her shoulder before dragging his tongue over her.

"I hope you don't have any plans today." His voice was still raw and unused. "'Cause you're shit out of luck if you think I'm letting you leave this bed."

"Don't make promises you can't keep," she teased as his tongue dipped lower.

"I'm a man of my word, darlin'." And he was determined to prove just that.

***

A whole week in Ivy's bed and he was officially addicted. They'd both comfortably settled into domesticity, and he couldn't even pretend that he wasn't loving every second of it. Every day they would wake up in her bed, work, eat, snuggle on the couch, and then fall back into bed. Of course, there were other activities in between, mostly involving his hands on her.

It was Saturday and probably the first time in a week he'd not been glued to Ivy's side. And he already missed her.

Damn, I'm a pussy.

As he parked up just outside Brady's, he let out a deep breath. His arm was killing him. There was no doubt he'd overdone it recently. Ranch work was tough, combine that with a whole new set of physical activities he'd added to his schedule, it was no wonder he was starting to feel the effects.

He jumped out of the truck, where his boots were met by the crunch of the gravel. To his surprise, he didn't need to bother with the doorbell. The red wood door swung open before he'd even reached the step.

"Ace!" Alice beamed, "I didn't know you were dropping by today."

Before he had a chance to reply, she was wrapping herself around him. She was a hugger. He'd learned that early on. When Brady had first introduced them, it was post-injury, and most people were too afraid to approach Ace. Not Alice though. She'd flung herself into his arms upon first sight and giddily squeezed him, all the while telling him how excited she was to finally meet Brady's blood brother. Her lack of boundaries was one of the qualities he loved most about her. That and she didn't seem to give a damn about what anyone thought of her.

"Hey, darlin', sorry I didn't call."

She pulled back and studied him for a moment, tucking her long dark hair behind her ear. "What's wrong? Something's wrong. You look weird."

He chuckled at her conclusion. "Nothing's wrong, I swear. Actually, if you must know, I'm pretty damn good." His thoughts drifted back to Ivy. He couldn't wait to get back home to her.

Goddamn, I'm one lucky son of a bitch.

"Oh, I see how it is." Alice crooked an eyebrow. "Come to brag to Brady that you're finally getting some?"

"Um … no! Fucking hell, Ali." He almost choked on his tongue. Where did she come up with this stuff? "I'm here to see you actually. My arm has been playing up; it's stiffer than usual. And seeing as my best friend's wife is the best physical therapist in town, thought I'd pick your huge, extremely intelligent, very attractive brain." He offered her a cheeky wink. Hoping flattery would get him everywhere.

Alice let out a snort. "Okay, okay, you can stop now. Get your arse inside and I'll take a look."

Fucking A.

He followed her inside and into their newly decorated living room. The first time he'd visited Brady here, there'd only been a solitary couch and a television. That was it. Minimalism at its finest. Since Alice had moved in, though, she'd worked her magic on every room in the house. Now there was not only furniture, but nice furniture. The comfiest of which, the large L-shaped navy couch, he deposited himself onto.

He looked around at the other touches, which had Alice's name written all over them. Matching armchairs, two chunky wooden coffee tables, and a huge shelving unit filled to the brim with books. The freshly painted walls were cream with the exception of one statement wall, which was a light gray. She'd done a hell of a job. She'd made this place into a home. It made him think of the ranch. Of Ivy. If money wasn't an issue, he wondered what kind of changes Ivy might make to her house.

"Okay, let's take a look." Alice scooted next to him and had already started to tug at his jacket.

"Jesus, woman, I can get my own jacket off. Sheesh." Ace grumbled, ignoring Alice's laugh.

Once he'd shrugged off the leather, he outstretched his arm in front of him and waited for Alice to finish up her inspection. She took her time, instructing him to bend and move it at certain angles while her fingers explored and she peppered him with questions.

"You still doing your exercises?"

"Not so much. I figured with all the manual labor I'm putting in at Moonrock, it would kinda balance out."

Alice shot him a look that clearly conveyed how very wrong he was. "I love you, Ace, but sometimes you really are a dumbass." She shook her head. "Right. Resume the daily stretches. And I think massages will help with the stiffness. Nothing fancy, a daily five-minute rub will do the trick and get the circulation pumping. Maybe Ivy could help you with that?" A smile started to curve up at the corners of her mouth.

Ace didn't say anything. Which he soon regretted. If he had said something, maybe he could have prevented the next words from leaving Alice's lips.

"Oh, so *now* you're shy? Does my lack of cock exclude me from getting all the dirty details? I know there's something going on with you and Ivy, and I'm not talking about that fake fiancé bullshit."

"Goddamnit, Ali. Can you not say *cock* in my presence? My fucking ears are bleeding." And they were. With Brady being practically a brother to him, Alice was the nearest thing he had to a sister. And that word was the last thing a man wanted to hear coming out of their sister's mouth. "Since when were you so interested in my sex life anyway?"

Bowling over with laughter, she was obviously finding the horror he was blatantly displaying on his face hilarious.

"I think you actually blushed, Ace. Freaking blushed!"

He scowled at her. "Fine, Ali. We're sleeping together. Happy?"

"Uh, yeah. 'Bout frigging time. You haven't been able to take your eyes off her since that day she turned up here. I'm not stupid, Ace. Neither is Brady. It was obvious to both of us that you were smitten."

So much for being subtle. Apparently he hadn't hidden a thing. There was at least one silver lining to having Alice all up in his business. He could actually prise some advice out of her. He still had no clue what he was doing with Ivy. They'd both expertly dodged the subject of what was happening between them. He didn't know how to do this. How to solidify things.

Over the next hour, he picked Alice's brain and sought out as much relationship advice as she was willing to share. It turns out having a sister is pretty damn handy.

CHAPTER NINE

"Is this okay?" Ivy waved the bottle of moisturizer in her hand at Ace.

He was waiting on the couch for her, looking fine as hell with one shirt sleeve rolled all the way up. When he'd told her he needed her help with his arm, she'd tried her hardest to reign in her shock. Even a week into their now very intimate relationship, he was still weird about his burns. Ivy couldn't understand it. She'd seen every part of him. Touched every inch. Kissed every inch. But still, it felt like he was holding back with her.

"Yeah, that'll do." His smile didn't reach his eyes. Great. He was already drawing into himself.

Bouncing down next to him, she pretended she didn't notice the flinch as she reached out for his arm.

It's not you. It's his scars.

The familiar reminder hit her stomach like a punch to the gut. Asking her for help was a start at least.

"So … I called Ali, to get some advice."

"Come again?" That got his attention.

"On the massage, I mean. I just didn't want to mess it up. I want to do this right."

Ace's face gentled, and she wondered what on earth he'd

thought she was speaking to Alice about. "Thank you, sugar, but you don't have to worry about messing anything up. It's just a quick rub to get the circulation going."

Her fingertips lightly grazed his skin, and she immediately felt him tense up under her touch. Reaching for a couple of her new satin throw pillows, she gently placed them underneath Ace's arm so he could try to relax a little.

Turning her whole body toward him, she pulled her legs up and sat cross-legged. Once she was comfortable, she squeezed a dollop of moisturizer into the palm of her hand. Using her cream-free hand, she laced her fingers through his and held his arm in place while she began to massage in the cream.

She started at his bicep and slowly worked her way down. It was true that touching Ace like this was no hardship. The mottled skin only served as a reminder of the type of man he was. A man who'd served his country. That man was brave. Strong. A survivor. And she was lucky enough to wake up in his arms every morning.

"This is nice. I like touching you like this. Do I get to do this every day for you?"

"Trust me, darlin', there's nothing that I want more than your hands on me daily. But I can think of far more preferable places for them." A wink and a smirk later, she was well aware of what he was doing. Brushing her off. Avoiding another real conversation about his scars.

"Well, those places will just have to wait until after I've taken care of your arm."

"Ivy, you don't need to take care of me. In fact, I can do this myself; it's fine." He tried to pull away, but she squeezed the hand she was still clinging onto.

That was it. No more.

"Ace. Stop." She waited patiently for him to meet her eyes again. When he did, she could see the hardness there. A deep blue ocean of pain. "I've tried not to push you. I've let you change the subject. Let you go quiet. Never ever called you out on your bullshit. But enough is enough. It's time."

"Time for what?" As if he didn't know.

"We need to talk about it. Your injury. What happened. Why you flinch every time I touch one of your scars outside of the bedroom. I'm done walking on eggshells. I need you to talk to me."

It was a ballsy move. She knew she had no right to make such a demand. She wasn't his girlfriend. They'd only been sleeping together a week and, really, she didn't know where she stood at all. What they were. Sure, there were plenty of labels she could put on them. Each one more complicated than the last. Roommate, fake fiancé, first man she'd slept with in five years.

He'd gone quiet. Keeping hold of him, she went back to massaging his arm, hoping like hell he wouldn't shut down on her.

It must have been a solid five minutes before he spoke again.

"What do you want to know?" His voice was flat, just like the line of his mouth. Devoid of any emotion she had no doubt was storming within him.

She cleared her throat. "How did it happen?"

The only giveaway he was affected by the question was the slight tick of his jaw. He was good, she'd give him that.

"We were in Afghanistan. My buddy Logan and I had been sent out on a convoy." Ace paused to run his free hand through his hair.

Ivy knew that it must be hard. Reliving it. But she had a feeling he needed to say it out loud just as much as she needed to hear it.

"Just as we were approaching the airfield, out of nowhere, this car hit us. Ran straight into us. I don't remember much after that. It kinda went black."

"Do you know how you got out or what happened after the car hit you?"

She ignored his now-bouncing thigh and continued to stroke him. She needed to touch him. Soothe him.

79

"The car was a bomb. The force of the blast flipped the vehicle over and I was knocked unconscious straight away. But I know Logan was the one who dragged me out of the burning truck. He saved my life." Ace let out a humorless laugh. "And I guess you're already familiar with my injuries." He lifted the arm Ivy was still massaging.

It was true—she could see the superficial wounds, but she was much more interested in the ones buried much deeper.

"Other than the burns … did you …?" She couldn't quite come up with the right words and trailed off.

"No." He cut off her chain of thought. "Other than the burns, I got lucky. I was treated for smoke inhalation, concussion, and a few fractures. No internal damage."

She refrained from agreeing that he was lucky. "The medical discharge was because of your burns then?"

Another flinch. "Yeah," Ace croaked. He mumbled the word "mobility," which she could only assume was his attempt at an explanation.

Releasing his arm, she removed the cushion barrier and climbed on top of his lap. She needed the closeness. The thought of him waking up in a hospital bed confused and alone made her chest feel tight. Resting her forehead against his, she slowly breathed him in. His usual musky scent was muddled with the whiskey he'd downed just after dinner.

They stayed like that for a while, both their eyes firmly shut. Once she felt ready to open them again, she stole a quick kiss before pulling back to get a better look at him.

"Thank you. For telling me. Can I ask you one more thing?" Ivy waited for him to nod before she continued. "Why won't you let me touch you? Even when we are … y'know … I can feel you tense up."

She was mentally preparing herself for a grunt or another non-answer when Ace surprised her. Blue flames burned into her as he caught her gaze, and she felt the intensity radiate through every fiber of her being.

"When you touch them, I remember all the reasons why

I shouldn't be touching you. Why I'll never be good enough for you. You have to know that I'm broken, Ivy. A part of me will always be missing. It was taken from me that day."

Speechless was probably not the right word to describe how she was currently feeling. Nevertheless, no words left her lips. She didn't know how she was supposed to take that. Was that his way of ending things? Or was he telling her that things between them weren't going anywhere? She was starting to wish he'd just grunted.

"Ivy. Say something."

After his last statement, she'd broken eye contact and was in no rush to look back up. She'd unrelatedly developed an interest in Ace's flannel shirt, more specifically, the buttons on it.

"Ivy." He practically growled.

"I just … I don't know what I'm supposed to say to that, Ace." The buttons were still fascinating. "Are you … I mean, are you saying … do you want to stop doing what we're—?"

Her words came to halt when he tilted her chin up, forcing her to meet his stare. "No way in hell do I want to stop what we're doing. You asked me why and that's the only answer I have for you. Yeah, I'm not good enough for you, but that doesn't mean I want this to end. You have to understand, I'm a selfish bastard, Ivy. I want you. All of you. And now that I have you, the last thing I'm gonna do is let you get away."

Despite a nagging feeling that those words were going to come back to bite her eventually, she felt somewhat placated by his explanation.

"Okay," was the only thing she could say.

Thankfully any further conversation was cut short by his lips capturing hers. It wasn't one of those times he was gentle and soft. No. This kiss screamed of pure possession. He was showing her just how much he wanted her. And in return she was going to show him just how much him opening up meant to her.

***

A date. Really, it was absurd. They'd already seen each other naked. Woken up together every morning and done very questionable things on her couch. Yet here she was, fretting over a date like some sort of freaking teenager.

To be fair, it had been a really, really long time since she'd been taken out. Dating hadn't exactly been an option over the past few years, not that she had men knocking down her door or anything. And if she did, she wouldn't have noticed. The ranch always came first.

After one last inspection of her outfit, she fluffed her hair and left the confines of her bedroom. She tried her hardest not to break an ankle in her heels as she made her way down the stairs. Making for a very slow descent. As she neared the bottom, she broke her concentration momentarily to look up and was shocked to find Ace there. Staring.

Don't trip. Don't trip. Don't trip.

Her face must have displayed her inner panic as one second later Ace was in front of her and offering her his hand. Touching him didn't help her concentration. Nor did being this close to him. He never failed to make her squirm. But in a suit. Squirm wasn't the word. More like quiver.

"I gotta say, sugar, you're looking mighty fine tonight." Ace shot her a smoldering smile.

"You don't look so bad yourself." That was putting it mildly.

Only one step down from her, he took advantage of them being eye level by laying a soft kiss on her lips. Proving once again that he could scramble her mind with ease.

She fought the urge to pout when he drew back. But the heat in his eyes was unmistakable. At least he was just as affected as she was.

"Sugar," he rumbled in that sexy bedroom voice, "you need to stop looking at me like that before I change my mind, take you upstairs, and rip that pretty little dress off you."

Sounds like a good fucking plan to me.

She didn't know at what point her inner voice had gotten so slutty, but she was blaming Ace. Standing there looking all manly and rugged. It was a miracle she wasn't drooling.

Suppressing the urge to jump him, Ivy decided to change the subject to something safer. "You never told me where we were going tonight."

Ace helped her down the last step and kept hold of her hand as he led them toward the door. "Brady told me about this nice Italian place over in Splitrock; I made us a reservation."

"Ooo, a reservation. Sounds fancy." Ivy wasn't kidding. She had never been anywhere where you had to book a table.

She came to a sudden halt as they made their way over to the truck. Gravel and heels did not go well together.

"What's wrong?" Ace looked concerned as he turned to face her.

"Maybe I should change my shoes. I don't think they're very practical."

He looked down at her feet and slowly raised his head, revealing a huge grin.

"What's so fun—" She didn't get a chance to finish before she was airborne and safely tucked against his hard chest.

A short dress meant that her panties were now exposed to the cool, evening air. *Classy.* Something that Ace had noticed and was taking full advantage of as his grip slid down. Even though it had been a while since she'd been on a date, she was fairly certain that this was not normally how a first one went. Then again, she supposed normal first dates didn't include going to dinner with your fake fiancé.

Once he'd placed her in the passenger seat and buckled her in, he rounded the truck and settled in for the ride.

The car journey went by quickly, and much to her

surprise, her nerves dissipated as they fell into their normal rhythm. They discussed the ranch. The latest gossip Ace had got from Brady about the possibility of Lily being pregnant again. And Teddy's newfound obsession with fantasy football.

Before she knew it, they had arrived, and Ivy's fingers were laced with Ace's as they walked into the elegant Ciao Bella. While Ace spoke to the hostess, she took in the dining room. The three chandeliers were clearly set to dim as it was honestly quite dark in there. Each table had a solitary rose in a slim vase and three candles circling it. It was a good thing there was some additional lighting, otherwise she wasn't going to be able to make out the menu.

Just as she was contemplating the deterioration of her eyesight, Ace tugged at her hand. They were on the move again. He must have asked for the best table in the place because that's what she saw when they came to a standstill. A curved black leather booth facing a floor-to-ceiling window offering up a stunning view of the mountains.

They slid into the booth next to each other, and Ivy had to admit, lighting be damned, this was the most beautiful place she'd ever been.

"Ace, this place, this view … I don't know what to say. It's perfect." She twisted to face him. "Y'know, I'm pretty sure Dotty's diner is just not gonna cut it after this."

His throaty laugh echoed around the quiet room, and she used the opportunity to slide closer to him. Pressing her thigh against his, she smiled as he turned that mischievous grin her way.

"Darlin', you wanna eat here every damn day, then you will." His eyes twinkled in the candlelight.

"Oh yeah?"

"Yeah. I don't think you fully understand just how gone for you I am. You want daily visits to Ciao Bella, done. You want flowers and jewelery, I'm on it. You want Christmas in Hawaii, tell me and I'll book it."

His expression had gone from playful to deadly serious

so fast, she was starting to question if he really had been laughing only a moment ago.

Gone for you. He's gone for me. Holy shit.

How was she supposed to eat when her stomach felt like a swarm of butterflies was having a party?

"Y-you …" *Great, I'm back to stuttering.* "Wanna take me to Hawaii?"

His callused fingers came up to her cheek and traced the line down to her lips. "I'll take you wherever you wanna go. Whatever you want, it's yours. Always."

"You a secret millionaire or something?"

Ace chuckled but kept his eyes on her. "No, not a millionaire, but I'm not hurting either. So, you want something, you tell me."

She was about to declare that she couldn't be bought when the waiter arrived with a bottle of wine. Wine that Ace had apparently already ordered for them. Realizing she hadn't even looked at the menu yet, she quickly scanned it while the wine was being poured. It didn't take her long to spot the creamy carbonara goodness that was calling out to her, so she was prepared when the waiter asked if they were ready to order.

Once they'd got in their requests, she turned her attention back to Ace, who was already sipping on the deep-red liquid. "You know I'm not interested in money, right? I don't want you to buy me jewelery or take me on expensive holidays. That's not the kinda girl I am. I ride horses, eat greasy diner burgers, and buy most of my clothes at the ranch and home supply store."

She watched as he placed his glass back on the table and moved his large hand toward her face again. This time he cupped her cheek. His expression soft.

"Sugar, I know exactly who you are. Trust me. Everything about you is perfect. And you may not want fancy gifts or holidays, but that doesn't mean you don't deserve them. You deserve the world, Ivy. And I will do anything within my power to give it to you."

Wow. Just wow.

Was this man for real? Was there a chance she was dreaming? Or perhaps in some sort of coma? Not only was he pure sex, but he was a romantic too.

As the night went on, she learned even more about Ace. In between slurping her creamy sauce, she listened intently as he relayed stories of his time as a marine. All the places he'd been to had her head spinning, especially as she'd never so much as left the country. It also had her questioning.

"Bluestone must feel really small to you," she blurted.

Ace eyed her curiously. "What do you mean?"

"I mean, you've been to all these places, seen all these things … lived in a huge city. Why on earth would you want to settle down in Bluestone, of all places?" *Why is my heart beating so fast?*

Ivy grabbed her wine glass and wasted no time taking a huge gulp as Ace pondered the question. He didn't leave her hanging for long though.

"Those places aren't going anywhere," he calmly stated. "If we wanna take a vacation, they'll be waiting for us, but right now I'm much more interested in making a home for myself. And Bluestone is the kinda town I could see myself doing just that."

We. Us. Home.

The pounding in her heart began to slow but the questions didn't. "You planning on making a home in one of my ranch cabins?"

It was now glaringly obvious that Ace wasn't short on funds. If he wanted a home, he could buy one. He didn't need to work for her in exchange for free rent.

"Not the cabin, no." He grinned. "But Moonrock, well that's a different story." Back was the hammering of her heart. "Let's just say … there is one thing in particular there that very much feels like home."

Is it physically possible to swallow your own tongue?

She was not going to survive this man. She realized right then and there, he would break her. In only a short space of time she'd fallen hard, and she had no idea if she was going to be able to get back up.

CHAPTER TEN

Ace had just finished putting everything away in the tack room when his phone vibrated again. This had to be the fourth time in five minutes. Only now, he had no excuse not to answer.

Pulling it from his jean pocket, he let out a sigh as he read the name.

"Hi, Ma, everything okay?"

"Okay? No, Ace, I'm not okay. My son has not only moved halfway across the country, but he also seems to have forgotten how to pick up the phone!"

He was starting to remember why he hadn't called. He'd faced down terrorists, gunfire, and car bombs, yet there was still nothing scarier than being on the wrong side of his mother. And it would appear that she was just about ready to pitch a hissy fit.

"Sorry, Ma, I've been meaning to call. I just got a little busy."

"Don't *sorry Ma* me, if you're really sorry, you'll get your butt on a plane and come visit your mama."

This was exactly why he'd escaped to Bluestone in the first place. Living in Texas was fine when he was on active duty. Seeing his family in small doses in between deployments was one thing, but after his medical discharge he'd felt suffocated by all their fussing.

"Like I said, I'm a little busy right now, Ma. I got a job at a local ranch, and I've got commitments."

"A ranch? Since when? You wanna do ranch work, your uncle Ronnie has a perfectly decent spread over here, and he's always looking for ranch hands. I'll give him a call."

"No, Ma, don't give Uncle Ronnie a call. I live here now, remember?" Ace's patience was beginning to wane. "I know it's hard, but you need to get used to it. In fact, why don't you and Dad come visit me up here?"

He regretted the invitation just as quickly as it left his lips. But it was too late. There was no way in hell his mother was going to miss a chance to see her son.

Ace winced as a squeal erupted over the line. "I'm booking tickets now, sweetie. What's the weather like there? It's cold I'll bet. And I take it you'll pick us up from the airport … or shall we rent a car? Are you staying on a ranch …? Do you have space for us, or should I book a room somewhere nearby?"

As his mom continued to sprout off questions, there was only one thing on his mind: Ivy. Even being new to this whole relationship thing, he was fairly certain it wasn't all right to invite your parents over to stay at your girlfriend's place without asking first. Especially when said girlfriend hasn't officially agreed to be your girlfriend yet. Then there was the whole fake fiancé thing. There was no way that little treasure wouldn't come back to slap him in the face in a town as small as Bluestone.

"I'll pick you up from the airport, and yes, you can stay here." Footsteps approaching caught his attention. He looked up to find Ivy staring at him. A puzzled look on her pretty face. "Gotta go, Ma. Text me over your flight info."

Once he'd hung up and tucked his phone back into his pocket, he immediately tugged Ivy into him. When she opened her mouth to say something, he cheekily took advantage and helped himself to a taste. Inhaling her sweet scent, a groan emanated from his throat. He could taste honey and sunshine. Heaven.

Her eyes were glassy when she finally pulled back, and he couldn't help but smirk. He did that to her. Him. "Uh … who's staying here?"

Shit. Focus. How do I do this?

"I sorta, might've, definitely did … invite my parents over. To stay here. With us."

Smooth.

Ivy's eyes widened. "You what? When?" That was definitely a panic-filled squeak.

His hands instinctively went to her face to offer her comfort. Stroking a stray wisp of hair back behind her ear, he locked eyes with her.

"I'm sorry, sugar. I know I should have asked you first. The invite just sorta slipped out. And once it was out there … well, I couldn't take it back. Let's just say my mama's not the kind of woman you wanna upset."

Ivy visibly gulped. "Don't you think she's gonna be mighty upset when she thinks you got engaged without telling her?"

The woman had a point.

"Maybe we could just tell her the truth … or maybe it won't even come up. Whatever happens, I'm sure it'll be fine." *Are you though?*

Ivy still looked unsure, but she simply nodded and said okay.

Ace was yet to let her go. His hand had stayed firmly in place and was now cupping her face while his thumb grazed over her cheek. Her skin was like silk. So smooth. So perfect. He couldn't wait any longer to ask her. It was time. He needed to make things official before she had a chance to change her mind.

"Sugar?" A smile formed as she visibly relaxed beneath his touch.

"Yeah?"

"There was something I've been meaning to ask you."

As their gazes remained entwined, the nerves started to creep in. What would he do if she said no? What if this was all too complicated for her? *And I'm too much of a freak.* "Uh. I booked another table at Ciao Bella's for us next week. And I thought we'd check out the French bistro in town tonight. Oh, and Brady said there was a movie theatre not too far from here, I thought we could check that out too."

Well done, man. You just asked her out on three dates and freaked her the fuck out.

"Um … okay," she said slowly, looking every bit as confused as he was right now. Why was this so hard? It was just a question. A question guys ask women all the time.

Before he could mess this up even more, he blurted it out. "Will you be my girlfriend?"

It was not smooth. Or romantic. And realizing where they were currently standing, it probably wasn't the best place to ask her either. A barn. Filled with horseshit.

Ivy blinked a few times before her smile grew even wider. The tightness in Ace's chest began to ease as he took in the sight of her. "Yes, Ace. Yes, I'll be your girlfriend," was all she said before flinging her arms around his neck and tiptoeing until her mouth met his.

Fucking A.

***

"So let me get this straight." Brady chugged down another gulp of his beer before narrowing his eyes on Ace. "Your parents are coming here to Bluestone. Like soon. Really soon. And you still haven't told them about Ivy. Oh and there's a good chance they're gonna hear about your fake engagement as soon as they step foot in town?"

Ace looked around Mickey's and made sure Teddy wasn't in earshot. "Yeah, that about covers it. So … you got any words of wisdom?"

At this point he'd take any advice that he could get. His mother wasn't joking when she told him she was booking flights straight away. They would be over in a matter of days.

"Yeah. Grow a pair and call your mom right now. Explain that you and Ivy are together *before* she gets here. And you might as well tell her about the fake engagement, try and explain it, y'know … that you're doing it for the business. Unless you wanna lie to your mom and face her scary-as-shit wrath when she finds out the truth?"

Ace sniggered into his whiskey glass. "You remember my ma, huh?"

"You kidding me? That woman is fucking terrifying, how could I forget."

That she was. She could also start a fight with an empty room. Brady was right. Ace needed to suck it up and call her. Now was as good a time as any. Downing what was left of his whiskey, he shot up from the table.

"Right. I'm gonna go call her before I wuss out. Wish me luck."

"Good luck, man. Another round for when you get back?" Brady gestured to his now-empty glass.

"Hell yeah. I'm gonna need it."

Making his way through the crowd, Ace drowned out the latest country track bellowing from the old jukebox and tried to think of what he was going to say. Once he'd made it to the alley next to Mickey's, he was still none the wiser. He was going to have to wing it.

Three rings later and his mouth was drying up. He was officially pathetic. A grown-ass man scared of his mother.

Always quick to answer, a few pleasantries later, and it was time for him to man up.

"Ma, there's something you should know before you get here."

"Okay, sweetie, what is it?"

He was silent for a moment as he gathered his thoughts. "The ranch where I'm staying … well, I'm living there with a woman. Ivy. She's my … she's my girlfriend."

His mother excitedly shrieked down the line. "Ace Robert Jones, you had me sweatin' like a hooker in church with that serious tone of yours! You're living with a woman? Sweet baby Jesus, thank the Lord. It's about damn time."

"Yeah, Ma, I am. It's new, but I really like her. And I think you will too. There is something else you should know though."

"Spit it out, sweetie, I'm not getting any younger."

"Well, the town sorta thinks we're engaged." The swift intake of breath he heard his mother taking had him blurting out the rest. "But we're not. See, Ivy's been having a bit of trouble with the ranch and having people think we're engaged has helped with business. I'll explain it all when you get here. I promise. But I need you and Dad to go along with it when you visit. Will you be able to do that for me?"

After a beat, his mom spoke again. "Okay, son, it's a little strange, but I'm sure you will tell us all about it when we come over. In the meantime, I'll warn your father."

That went much better than Ace thought it would go. His mom wasn't exactly a *go with the flow* type of woman, but apparently news of her son finally getting a girlfriend was enough to bring out a new calmer side of her.

Relief flooded him as he wrapped up the call. Now that was out of the way, he was actually looking forward to his parents visit and having them meet Ivy. He already knew they would love her. Who wouldn't?

"You fucking what?" Teddy's angry voice boomed from behind him.

Just ten seconds of relief, really? Sounds about fucking right.

Ace turned to find a six-foot-four ball of anger. Teddy's bulging, inked arms were crossed over his chest, and he looked about ready to rip him limb from limb.

"Teddy, look, before you—"

"Don't you fucking dare try and worm your way out of this. You're living with my sister, *sleeping* with my sister, and you're not actually fucking engaged? You both lied to me? To my fucking face?"

There was a lot of "fucking" in that little speech. Something told Ace that wasn't a good sign. It was a very,

very bad sign. Teddy was mad as hell.

"Let me explain …" The next words died in his throat as Teddy pushed him against the brick wall and got in his space. This was not going well. It wasn't like Ace was short. He was six-one. But it turns out those extra three inches Teddy had on him made quite a bit of difference when you pair it with a scowl and a dark corner.

"You hurt one hair on my sister's head, and I'll hunt you down and fucking gut you. You understand me?"

Now Ace was just plain pissed off. Enough with the threats already. He wasn't some scumbag only after one thing, and he didn't enjoy being treated like one. His feelings for Ivy were real. Frighteningly real. Also, since when does pretending to be someone's fiancé turn you into public enemy number one? Did Teddy miss the part about Ace trying to help her out?

"No offense. But fuck you, man." A menacing growl escaped Teddy's throat, but Ace ignored it and carried on. "If you think for one second I'd hurt Ivy, then you haven't been paying fucking attention. Yeah, you're right, we shoulda told you what we were doing, but that doesn't change the fact that we're together. And you need to get used to it. I'm not going anywhere. Ivy's mine. Now back the fuck off."

A lesser man might crumble under Teddy's glare. Ace, however, was over this conversation. He pushed away from the wall, with a look almost daring Teddy to make a move. The big man studied Ace for a while with the same serious expression on his face.

"Tell Ivy I'll be by tomorrow. You, me, and her have some talking to do."

Can't wait.

***

The next day, Ace found himself face to face with a scowling Teddy once again. This time they were sat across from each other, and Ivy was by his side. Her hand tenderly stroking his thigh as she attempted to diffuse the tension filling the kitchen.

She hadn't exactly been pleased when he'd returned home last night only to tell her about his chat with her brother. But after a ten-minute freak-out, she admitted that it was probably for the best. Ace knew how much she'd hated lying to him. So, in a way, it was a good thing. That's what he kept telling himself anyway.

"So, let me get this straight," Teddy bristled, "instead of doing the sensible thing like coming to me, *your family*, for actual financial help … you instead decide to pretend to be engaged to this fucking jarhead in the hope of luring back some sexist asshole clients. Is that right? Am I missing anything? Like the moment you lost your fucking sanity, Ivy?"

"Hey," Ace snapped, not liking the man's tone in the slightest, "don't fucking talk to her like that."

"She's my goddamn sister, asshat, I'll talk to her any damn way I like."

Ace pushed up from the chair, anger stinging his skin. Teddy wasted no time pushing up from his seat too, matching Ace's stance and staring him down.

"Enough!" Ivy intervened, pulling at Ace's arm until he complied and sat back down on the hard wooden stool. "Will you both just stop with the macho bullshit? Teddy. Sit down."

Sulkily, her brother did as she said. Leaning back into his chair, he crossed his arms over his chest and waited. He didn't have to wait long. Neither of them did. Ivy was just getting started.

"Look, Teddy, the reason I didn't come to you for help is because I'm embarrassed."

"Ivy—" Teddy started but was quickly cut off.

"Let me get this out, okay?" She waited for him to nod before continuing. "For years you've been ploughing money into Moonrock. And the amount you've put into it … hell, it must be enough to buy that damn bar you work in. Well, enough is enough. Somethings got to give. Another money injection from you will get me through the next few months, but then what? I need clients, Teddy. That's the only way the ranch will survive. *You* know it, *I* know it, *Ace* freaking knows it. So, yes, I decided to go along with the whole fake fiancé thing because why the hell not? I was all out of ideas. And you know what? It's working, Teddy. Believe it or not, it's *actually* working! I got an old client back and a brand spanking new one too!"

The smile that took over Ivy's face had Ace's chest squeezing. She was right, it was working. But Ace didn't think it was for the reason she thought it was. They had more meetings with new clients than old ones, which led him to believe that Ivy had just simply needed some help. Another body to share the workload with. That was all.

"Sis." Teddy's voice was soft as he shook his head in sadness. "I'm the one who should be embarrassed. You've been running a whole goddamn ranch on your own. I shoulda helped more. I didn't know how bad it had got. Why didn't you come to me, tell me, we could have worked something out? I coulda quit the bar and been here full time."

Reaching across the table, Ivy took hold of her brother's hand. "This isn't where you're supposed to be, Teddy. It's not where you're happy. And that's okay. I have to learn to do this on my own, and if I can't … well, then I can't. But I need to try. You get that, right?"

This talk had clearly been long overdue. Despite Ace feeling like the ultimate gate crasher for this honest sibling exchange, he reminded himself just why he was there. For Ivy. With that reminder, his palm went to Ivy's back and gently glided up and down her spine. If comfort was all he had to contribute to this conversation, then it would be the best damn comfort she ever had.

***

After successfully making it through a whole conversation with Teddy without either one of them throwing a punch, Ace was celebrating. He'd taken his woman to Dotty's diner and was currently treating her to her favorite greasy burger.

Their talk today had ended pleasantly. With a firm handshake and a nod of something like approval. Which was good because he meant what he said last night. Ivy was his and he wasn't going anywhere. Which meant he needed to play nice with Teddy.

"Penny for your thoughts?" Ivy beamed as she brought the burger back up to her mouth.

"I was just thinking about how well this morning went. You know, I was pretty sure your brother was gonna show up armed."

Ivy threw her palm up to her mouth to stifle her giggle. She was as cute as hell. He leaned back into the red leather booth seat and admired the view. He still couldn't believe she was his. He was one lucky man.

"He wouldn't shoot you. Well, not in front of a witness anyway." She smirked.

"That doesn't make me feel any better, sugar." He arched a brow at her, noticing that her smile only grew bigger.

"Anyway, enough about my family. You still haven't given me the lowdown on yours. Your parents get here in two days, and you haven't told me a thing about them, despite my numerous attempts trying to coerce information out of you."

The truth was there wasn't much to say. They were typical Southern parents. Protective. Slightly dysfunctional. And loud. Really loud.

"I'm not trying to dodge your questions. I promise. What do you wanna know?"

She took a moment to slurp on her chocolate milkshake before leveling him with those inquisitive eyes. "What's your mom like? Does she work, and if not, did she used to, or was she a stay-at-home mom? Does she have a favorite drink or food or anything really that I could stock up on?"

He couldn't help but chuckle. She wasn't joking when she said she had questions. "My ma is a straight talker, loud, a little overbearing but has a heart of gold. She's retired now, but she used to be an elementary teacher. As far as favorites are concerned, trust me when I say she will be bringing everything she needs … and a whole load of crap she thinks we need too."

"Why would she bring us stuff?"

Her innocent question caused a pang in his chest, reminding him of the stark differences in their childhoods. She didn't talk about her parents, and he never pushed the topic, but he knew she'd been just six years old when they'd died. Just the thought of her going through something so tragic, so young, cut him to his very core.

Reaching over the steel-topped table, he laced his fingers through hers. "She'll want to take care of us. Mother hen us. If you think you'll be able to lift a finger while she's here, you've got another thing coming."

"But … she's never met me. What if she hates me?"

"Darlin', trust me when I tell you she already loves you. And, sugar, there's not one damn thing to hate about you. You're perfect."

As if making his point, a pretty blush tinged her cheeks. *Yeah. I'm really fricking lucky.*

CHAPTER ELEVEN

Ace wasn't kidding when he said his mom would come prepared. They'd arrived a while ago and Ivy was still unpacking all the food and never-ending gifts Mr. and Mrs. Jones had shown up with.

"You really didn't have to do this." Ivy held up a plush satin throw, pulled from the latest bag. "Really, Mrs. Jones, you really shouldn't have. This is too much."

"For the millionth time, call me Liz," the older woman huffed, "and don't be silly, sweetheart, it's nothing. Just a few bits and pieces I thought you might like."

It was not nothing. It was five hundred thread count bedding, velvet throw pillows, and soft towels. The woman was redecorating a home she'd been in less than an hour. Ivy didn't know what to make of it. Should she throw herself into the woman's arms and thank her for gifting her with such beautiful things? Or should she be insulted that she assumed she lived in a house full of crap? Which she did, of course. But how was she supposed to know that?

Seeing as Ivy was head over heels for Liz's son, Ivy went with the first option.

"Thank you, Liz. Everything is just amazing. And really thoughtful."

Turns out Liz was a hugger. Within a split second, Ivy was thrust into her embrace. And it didn't feel bad. Maybe it was because it reminded her of her grandma's hugs. It had been almost nine years since she'd had one of those. Relaxing into Mrs. Jones' hold, Ivy openly accepted the motherly comfort and breathed in the notes of lavender of her perfume.

After a minute, Liz pulled back slightly, her hands going straight for Ivy's shoulders. "Ace told me about your parents, sweetie."

Suddenly, Ivy felt a knot start to twist in her stomach. She really did not want to have this conversation. She hadn't even had it with Ace yet, so she wasn't exactly jumping at the chance to tell his mother all about her depressing childhood.

Obviously unable to hide her discomfort, Liz's features softened, her light blue eyes looking almost misty. "I just meant you're not alone anymore, sweetie. You need anything at all, you tell me, okay? You wanna talk, we'll talk. You want homemade cookies, I'll whip some up for you."

You're not alone anymore.

Ivy needed to get the hell out of there, *pronto*. She was too damn close to having a full-scale emotional breakdown. Who knew she was so close to one in the first place? Just one hug and a promise of homemade cookies had tipped her over the edge.

And those words. That innocent promise from a virtual stranger, pulled at her heartstrings until they were all tangled up. She knew she wasn't really alone. She had Teddy. They'd always had each other. But losing their parents and then their grandparents had hit them both hard. The heartache hardening something in both of them. She often wondered if that was why they'd found themselves single in their thirties. Too afraid to let anyone in.

She must have looked as fragile as she felt because Liz hadn't uttered another word. Probably in fear Ivy would break. To be fair, she might.

Don't just stand there. Say something!

Before she could choke out some sort of thank you, Ace appeared at her side. His strong arm immediately tucking her into him, and she was shocked to discover that the small gesture made her feel better. Calm. Safe. When he dropped a kiss onto her forehead, she melted into his comfort even further.

"Ma, can you give us a second?"

Liz didn't say a thing and scurried out of the room, leaving them alone. Ace's hands were on Ivy again moments later, turning her to face him, a clearly concerned look clouding his features.

"You okay, sugar? Talk to me."

Words continued to fail her, but the tears? They spilled so fast; she didn't know they were dampening her cheeks until the sting of salt hit her lips. It was too late. The breakdown was happening. Right here. Right now. With Ace's parents in the next room.

Excellent timing, Ivy. Way to make a good first impression.

Ace's thumbs were swiping away the droplets as they fell. "Sugar, please. Tell me what's wrong. What can I do?"

This wasn't the time or the place to fall apart or explain to him why she was currently leaking. The story was too long. And too sad.

"I-I'm okay," she rather unconvincingly managed to stutter out. "I-I just need a minute and to splash some water on my face. That's all."

He studied her, clearly not agreeing with her assessment. "Why don't you go on upstairs, darlin'? I'll be there in a minute."

That seemed too easy. But she wasn't about to argue. She had a chance to run, and she was taking it. Scrambling up the staircase, she went straight into her bedroom and threw herself head-first into the pillow. Just one minute and then she would clean herself up.

She missed Ace coming in and taking a seat next to her on the bed. It wasn't until she felt the gentle caress of his fingers on her back that she was alerted to his presence. Instantly, she shifted and twisted to face him. He looked no less concerned than he had been downstairs.

"I'm okay now." She wasn't. "I'll make us lunch, and then maybe we can give your parents a tour of the ranch? Maybe take them out for a ride?"

Ace half smiled before climbing into bed next to her. Once he was lying on his back, he gathered her in his arms and positioned her head on his chest and her arm across his stomach.

"I sent my parents out for the afternoon; they'll be back later for dinner. It's just you and me. So … you gonna tell me what happened back there?"

She attempted to sit up but was quickly pulled back down into his hard chest. "Why did you do that? I'm fine, Ace. I swear. Your parents have only just got here, we should be with them."

He maneuvered them again until they were both facing each other. "No, sugar, you're not fine. And before I unleash my parents on you, I need to find out why and make it better. So, I'm gonna need you to talk to me, Ivy."

The sincerity and worry in his tone had her wanting to open up to him, but it wasn't that easy. She didn't know how to do this. How to share. He must have sensed as much, as he started to talk again.

"Why don't we start with what upset you downstairs?"

Ivy swallowed down the lump in her throat. She knew she needed to be honest. No more hiding. "Your mom was being so nice. And motherly. And she mentioned she knew about my parents and then said that I wasn't alone anymore, and I just lost it." She took a breath. "I'm sorry. Your mom must think I'm crazy."

Fierce eyes bore into her. "You've got nothing—not one damn thing—to be sorry for. You hear me?" His tone was firm and scarily serious. "I told you already, but I'll tell you again, my mom already loves you. She loves you because she knows what you mean to me. She knows if she's here meeting you, you're special. And she's right. You are. The last thing she thinks is that you're crazy or rude or whatever else that's swirling around in that head of yours. And y'know, I hate to say it, but she's right, you're not alone anymore. I know it's not been long, but now that I've found you, there's not a chance in hell that I'm letting you go."

Jesus. That was a lot. I don't know which part I like better.

Who was she kidding? She knew exactly which part of that little speech she liked the most. *I'm not letting you go.* His words, the deep husk of his voice, the unwavering affection he constantly surprised her with, she was putty in this man's hands. Suddenly opening up wasn't that frightening anymore.

"I don't really remember much about my mom and dad," she whispered, her attention darting to the stretched cotton over his chest. "Teddy remembers more than I do. He was older when they ..." She trailed off.

Ace lightly dragged his fingers up and down the curve of her waist in a soothing motion as she continued. "I remember that night though." She squeezed her eyes shut as she pictured the sheriff standing in her grandparents' hallway, hat in hand. "At the time I didn't really understand what was happening, but looking at my nana from the top of the stairs, through the railings, hearing her wail, seeing her collapse on the floor ... I just knew... I knew that nothing would ever be the same again."

Seconds later she was pulled back into Ace's chest. His big arms wrapped around her and held on to her tight. They lay like that for a while before Ivy was able to talk again. When she did, she remained in place, not ready to come out of her cocoon just yet.

"My nana raised me, and I'm so grateful for the life her and Pops gave me and Teddy but ... she was always just my nana, y'know? She wasn't a mom. *My* mom. I don't know what it's like to have a mom. I think that's why I didn't know how to act downstairs. Or what to say to your mom. I really am sorry I freaked out. I'll try harder."

She felt guilty admitting it out loud. Her grandparents took her and Teddy in and gave her the life she has now. Entrusted this ranch to her. They never pretended to be her parents, and she understood why.

But she'd always wondered how her life would be different if her parents' car hadn't crashed that fateful night. What it would have been like to have a normal childhood. A mother who fusses and an overprotective father. What would they have thought of the woman she grew up to be? What would they have thought of Ace?

"Sugar, I swear to God, if you apologize one more time, I'm gonna spank your ass. There is nothing for you to be sorry for. You understand me?"

Despite his reassurance, she was still mortified that Liz had witnessed her breakdown within only an hour of meeting her. Talk about a bad first impression.

"You really do need to work on your threats." Ivy smiled into his chest as he vibrated against her. She was happy she'd managed to lighten the mood.

Once his chuckles had subsided, Ace lay a soft kiss on top of her head. "You know … I'm pretty sure there's more than enough of my mother to go around. You wanna share?"

That made her smile wider. He was right. From what she had seen so far, there was more than enough.

"Did you see what she brought?" She leaned back slightly and brought her eyes back to meet his. "There's enough stuff there to redecorate at least half the house."

A hoarse snigger ripped through him. "Yeah, that doesn't surprise me. It's kinda what she does. And it's the first time she's been let loose to buy any type of girly shit. She's always had a house full of men. Me, my brothers, and my dad. Meeting you. Having you. Trust me, she's in heaven right now."

"Having me?"

"Yeah. She has you now. The daughter she always wanted."

"But ... I'm not ... I mean ..."

"Baby, what part of *I'm not letting you go* don't you get?" Ace's hands were moving again and had gone back to caressing her curves, his fingertips leaving a trail of goosebumps behind in their wake. "My ma's not dumb. The fact she's here meeting the woman I'm in a relationship with, living with, she knows what that means."

Was it getting hot in here? "What does that mean?"

"I've never introduced my ma to a girl. So, me wanting her to meet you ... sorta says it all."

Ivy changed her mind. That was enough information for her to process right now. She didn't need to know what "sorta says it all" meant. Actually, enough sharing. There was such a thing as too much sharing.

"Honey?" That particular endearment was usually reserved for bedroom-related activities, but there was no going back now. No holding back. Not after what she'd just shared. Plus, he started it by throwing out "baby" and making her feel all tingly.

"Yeah, sugar." Ace's gruff voice cracked.

"Kiss me."

She didn't have to ask him twice.

***

Last night, when Ace's parents returned to the ranch, no one mentioned Ivy's breakdown. In fact, Ace had made sure all topics of conversation centered around himself and his younger brothers only, for which she was grateful.

But today there was no escaping the impending scrutiny. Today, she was alone with his mother. Under the guise of a shopping trip, Liz had managed to whisk Ivy away from the safety of her ranch and her man.

They were alone in Bob's gift shop. Well, Bob was there, but he was as deaf as a doornail, so he might as well have not been. Liz was currently admiring a pair of glass tea candle holders, while Ivy was biting down hard enough on her lip to possibly draw blood.

"These would go nicely with those frames I brought over, don't you think?"

Ivy released her lower lip and cringed at the metallic taste now filling her mouth. "Uh, sure, I guess." She picked up the set and inspected the holders. "I should probably pick up some candles while we're here too then."

Liz let out a chuckle. "Sweetheart, you don't have to buy it because I like it."

I don't? Ivy's thoughts must have been written all over her face if the humor quickly draining from Liz's features was anything to go by. The older woman gave her shoulder a gentle pat. "Why don't you show me the kind of things you like, sweetie?"

Ivy silently cursed herself. She was really messing up this whole bonding thing. How was she supposed to know what to do or how to act in a situation like this? She'd never once met the parents of anyone she'd dated.

Trying to pull herself out of her head, Ivy led them over to the chrome plant pot stands that had caught her eye earlier.

"I like these. I mean, I'd have to buy an actual plant to put in them, but I think they would brighten up the living room."

"They're perfect, Ivy. We should get one. And then we should go get you that plant."

She couldn't help but smile. This was Liz's way of showing love. It was probably where Ace learned it from. He was constantly trying to spend money on her. Spoil her. It was all very new to her. She didn't know if she liked it yet. Things were just things. Actions were what really mattered.

After insisting she paid for the stand, they made their way to the home supply store to browse plants. Ivy was starting to have fun as she listened to Liz relay stories of a younger Ace. Ivy wasn't surprised at all about hearing how protective he was of his little brothers. There was only two years difference between Ace and Josh, while Reese was five years younger.

"My brother, Teddy, was the same." Ivy laughed. "Still is in fact. There's just three years between us, but he still treats me like a little girl made of glass."

They were now browsing the aisles of Greenways, and she'd immediately spotted a beautiful snake plant. Ivy headed straight toward it, and Liz was hot on her heels.

"It's an older sibling thing," Liz continued their conversation. "You'll see when you have kids of your own. Even if you have a girl first, she'll be just as protective of her younger brother or sister."

Ivy froze in place. Luckily she'd reached the snake plant, which was good because she didn't think she would be able to move even if she wanted to. Kids. When she has kids of her own? Does Liz mean with Ace? Does she think that's where Ivy and Ace are heading?

Fuck.

She was back to freaking out. Internally of course. Liz had seen enough of her crazy already. This is why Ivy had been single. Why she'd not actively sought out a relationship. There were certain expectations when it came to relationships at her age. Expectations that she'd never be able to live up to.

"You all right, sweetie?"

She swallowed down every emotion bubbling to the surface. "Uh, yeah. I was just thinking about where to put the plant. What do you think?"

One thing was for sure. She needed to distract Liz.

"Well, I think this right here would look perfect by those big bay windows of yours." She offered up a warm smile and tucked a strand of her short blonde bob behind her ear.

"I think so too," Ivy mused, her attention turning back to the waxy leaves. "I think this is the one." She picked up the pot and smiled at Liz.

"Me too, sweetie, me too."

***

Ivy burrowed her head deeper into Ace's chest. Two days with his parents had been surprisingly fun. But this right here, was the best part of the long weekend. In bed with Ace. His big arms wrapping around her felt like a security blanket she never knew she needed until now.

"I'm fairly certain my ma is gonna kidnap you and take you back to Texas with her."

Ivy didn't need to look up to know that he was smiling.

"I might just let her."

Ace's deep laugh made her head shake. "Oh, no, you don't, sugar. I'm keeping you here with me." His arms squeezed tighter around her. "I told you, I'm not letting you go. Not even if it's with my mother."

Ivy skimmed her fingers lightly over the mottled skin on Ace's chest. Ever since their talk about what happened the day of his injury, he'd started allowing her to touch him freely without tensing up or pulling her hand away. It had even brought them closer. As silly as it sounded, by letting her touch his scars, she felt like he was putting his trust in her. He was letting his guard down. Allowing himself to be vulnerable.

After laying kisses on his chest, she looked up to find Ace's eyes fixated on her. Drinking her in.

"What?" she inquired when his stare didn't waver.

"You're so fucking beautiful."

Ace was never stingy when it came to compliments. She should be used to it, but she wasn't. And it wasn't just the words either. It was the way he looked at her. The way he touched her. Kissed her. Made her feel like she was the most special person on the planet.

"How do you do that?"

"Do what?"

"Make me want to believe you."

Her honest admission caused her pulse to quicken, but before she had a chance to worry about that, strong hands went under her armpits. Ace tugged her up until they were face to face and she was under the scrutiny of those piercing eyes.

"Sugar, you should believe me." She melted at the sincerity in his husky voice. "Thirty-three years I've been on this earth, and I've never, not once, met anyone like you. Trust me when I tell you the beauty you have is rare. It starts from inside and shines brighter than the sun."

She wanted to bury her head back into his chest and hide from his words. From his compliments. From everything. But his hold kept her firmly in place. She could only gulp and wait for him to continue.

"You understand what I'm saying?"

She shook her head. She really didn't. There wasn't anything special about her. It wasn't that she was lacking in confidence. She knew she wasn't a complete car wreck. She was no model by any means, but with the right makeup she could pass for pretty decent.

"Look, Ace. I don't need romantic, flowery words. If you haven't already noticed, you have me. We're together. In and out of bed. And that's enough for me."

"That's not enough for me."

"What do you mean?"

"I mean, I need you to understand how beautiful you are. Inside and out. Don't get me wrong, I never thought I was the romantic, flowery-words type of guy. It was just as much a shock to me as it was to you I guess. But you seem to bring it out in me. And I need to be able to tell you how I feel."

She gulped again, feeling like the biggest bitch ever. Here was the hottest man she'd ever seen telling her how beautiful she was, and her insecurities were trying their hardest to shut it all down.

"Okay, honey," she whispered, "I'll try harder. I'm just not used to it, but I'll try. I really will."

By the look on his face, that didn't seem to be the right answer either. He looked positively murderous. She couldn't win.

"Listen to me, sugar." His big hand was now encompassing half her face. "I don't want you to try to do anything. That's not what I meant. You're perfect. You don't need to change a damn thing. I'm sorry if that's how it came across. What I meant was I want to be able to tell you how beautiful you look or how happy you make me whenever I feel like it. But if it's too much or you're uncomfortable, you tell me, okay?"

Yep, it's official. I'm a bitch.

"Okay, honey." In an attempt to wipe that serious expression off his face, she kissed him. And thankfully, he kissed her back.

CHAPTER TWELVE

Ace sat across from his mother and father in Dotty's diner. Ivy hadn't joined them. She'd insisted he have some alone time with his parents before their flight back this afternoon. Ace didn't think it was necessary. As far as he was concerned, now that she was a part of his life, they should both get used to doing the whole family time thing together. But he hadn't wanted to argue with her. Which was why he was there without her, eating eggs and missing her like crazy. Like a lovesick fool.

"So, when's the wedding?" His ma asked with a wide-eyed grin.

"Very funny."

His mother sure was embracing the whole fake engagement thing. When strangers came over to congratulate her, she wasted no time telling them all about the huge, lavish wedding she was planning while his dad rolled his eyes. At one point, she'd even announced that they would be starting a family very soon. That little tidbit had obviously scared the crap out of Ivy, as all the color in her face had instantly drained.

"Actually, I'm being serious. You already got her the ring, which I might add, is stunning. Who knew my son had such good taste?" She took another sip of her coffee but kept her eyes firmly on him.

He looked to his dad for help, but he simply shrugged. Great. He was on his own.

"Ma, I'm not having this conversation."

"Why not? You seem to be having it with the whole town day in and day out. You can't have it with your own mother?"

Ace let out a heavy sigh. "It's still early days, Ma. Can you wait until we've been together at least a few months before you marry us off?"

His mother's husky chuckle caught the attention of half the diner. When she finally stopped, she placed a hand on his father's lap and smiled up at Ace.

"She's the one, son. I know it. You know it. Your father knows it. But to answer your question. Yes. I can wait a few more months before I announce your engagement. The real one."

She's the one.

He didn't have a reply for that. Was Ivy the one? It sure felt like it. But he didn't have much to compare their relationship to. He'd never been in love. How was he supposed to recognize it if it came along? As if reading his thoughts, his mother reached across the shiny silver table and covered her palm over his forearm.

"Take all the time you need. You'll know when you'll know. Not a second sooner. But in the meantime, for the love of God, don't let her slip away. You understand me?"

Ace unconsciously nodded. He had no intention of letting her go. It had taken him thirty-three years to find her. He was holding on tight.

After a minute, he announced, "She's the one." He knew what admitting that meant. He should be scared shitless, but for some reason, saying it out loud felt good. It felt like the first step to a happy life. With Ivy.

His mother was understandably beaming. It was his father's reaction that he wasn't prepared for. His normally stoic dad was misty-eyed. And after a short and sharp clearing of his throat, he offered up his opinion for the first time.

"I knew the second I laid my eyes on your mother, that I wanted to spend the rest of my life with her. Now I know times change and all that, but being here with you, seeing you and Ivy together … I recognize that same look in your eyes, son. And I'm happy for you. I really am. She's an incredible woman. Just like your mother."

This wasn't how Ace had expected breakfast to go, that was for sure. But he couldn't deny the approval his parents had for his relationship with Ivy felt damn good. They'd recognized the special. And had known even before him that she was the one. He was lucky to have them. And lucky to have Ivy. Now all he had to do was not fuck it up.

***

It had been just a few weeks since his parents visit and in that time not only had Ace and Ivy's relationship grown stronger but so had the business. Which was why Ace wasn't the least bit surprised to see Donoghue's obnoxiously expensive truck currently making its way up Moonrock's gravel driveway.

Ace crossed his arms over his chest and watched as the older man parked and exited his vehicle. What he wouldn't give to wipe that arrogant smirk off his face.

Unfazed by Ace's icy demeanor, Donoghue didn't bother formerly greeting him and simply nodded in his direction before asking, "Ivy around?"

The nerve. "What do you want?"

"I'd like to speak with Ivy," he repeated.

"And I'd like world peace, but it ain't fucking happening. What do you want, Donoghue?"

Ace watched the plump man puff out his now-red cheeks. "I have another offer for her."

"She's not interested."

"Don't you think *she* should be the one to decide that?"

"What's the matter, Donoghue … you not liking dealing with men so much anymore?"

Ace didn't feel the least bit bad for making the graying man before him squirm. What he'd said to Ivy was unforgivable. Ace had no doubt the man was behind the steady loss of Moonrock's clients in the years since Ivy's grandfather had passed.

Ignoring Ace's dig, the old man didn't seem to know when to give up. "I'm prepared to double my original offer."

"No."

"Think about it."

"Okay, let me think." Ace mockingly stroked the stubble dotted around his chin. "No. Now, leave."

"Listen, son, this will be my last offer. I suggest you take it. Because when foreclosure comes knocking on your door, I might not be feeling so generous."

Foreclosure? Ace felt like laughing in the old man's face. His contact at the Splitrock Bank obviously hadn't informed him of the recent deposits he and Ivy had been making. Likely due to the formal complaint Ivy submitted to the branch manager not long after their first meeting. The most important thing was, though, that the ranch was no longer in danger of closing. So Donoghue's threats were emptier than that big bulbus head of his.

"Noted. Now, do I need to get the shotgun, or are ya gonna get the hell off our drive?"

Ace watched patiently as Donoghue cursed under his breath before climbing back into his truck. Once he was safely out of sight, Ace went in search of Ivy. It had been far too long since he'd held her for his liking.

As soon as he caught sight of her leaving the barn, his heart swelled. Her hair was braided, and she was in her signature jeans and tank, with a chequered shirt hanging open. Beautiful. He was no longer scared of what he was feeling for her. He knew it was fast, but it was right. She was right.

After admitting to his parents that he thought she was the one, the past few weeks had only cemented his feelings. Ace had taken her out whenever she allowed it. Although, if it were up to Ivy, they wouldn't leave the bedroom. Not that he was complaining. He'd realized after the first time they went to bed together that he'd never be able to get enough of her.

"Hey, honey."

He loved it when she called him honey. But it was her smile that hit him full force in the chest as she made her way over to him.

"Hi, sugar." As soon as she was close enough, he pulled her flush against his chest and dipped his head down to take her lips. After a quick taste, he pulled back, not wanting to get carried away. But he kept her close and let his fingers trail down the contours of her face. "I missed you."

Ivy scoffed. "Yeah, right. It's been an hour, Ace."

"An hour too long." He grinned back at her. "So … we had a visitor."

"Yeah? Who?"

He still hadn't let her go and didn't intend to. "Donoghue. Apparently he wants to double his offer."

"I bet he does." She sniggered. "I take it you told him where to go?"

"Damn straight."

With Evan's business and the new clients Ace had scored after speaking to a few of his brother's rodeo contacts, it wouldn't be long until Moonrock was back in profit and Ivy would never have to think about Donoghue again. She wouldn't even have to carry on doing business with the likes of Thomas Weston if she didn't want to.

"Oh, I forgot to tell you." Ivy jumped up and down in his hold. "Tomorrow night we've been invited over to Jake and Lily's. They're having some sort of dinner party and I said we'd go. That okay?"

As if she even needed to ask. "Of course, sounds good. Who else is going?"

"Well, Brady and Alice, and I think Jake's sister, Sam, and her fiancé, Duke. I guess it's like a couples thing."

"Good thing we're a couple then." He couldn't wipe the happy from his face even if he tried.

"Yeah, honey, it's a good thing." Those emerald eyes sparkled as she tiptoed up to meet his lips. Just when he thought his day couldn't get any better, he got another taste of heaven.

***

Something was going on with Ivy. They'd only been at Jake and Lily's ranch for an hour, and he'd watched her slowly draw into herself. When they'd first arrived, the women had congregated in the kitchen while the guys had stayed in the living room to watch Jake's little girl, Hayley.

Now they were all in one room, but as Hayley had taken quite a shine to Ace, he had his hands full. Therefore, he was unable to pull Ivy to one side and find out what was going on. Every time he'd tried to pass Hayley back to Jake or Lily, she'd scream the house down. Which was why he was currently stuck rocking a gurgling baby. Not that he minded. She was adorable. And having her in his arms, he couldn't help but think about having one of his own one day. With Ivy.

His stomach groaned as mouth-watering smells started to trickle into the room. Dinner was ready. A fact Lily announced just minutes later.

With the help of Jake, they eventually got Hayley settled down for a nap while everyone else disappeared into the dining room. Once he'd finally taken his place next to Ivy around the large pine table, he was no less concerned. She was giving off weird vibes.

Throughout the meal, he tried numerous times to find out what was wrong, but she'd only shrug him off and insist she was fine. She wasn't fine. That, Ace was sure of. She hadn't been herself since they'd arrived. She was definitely hiding something behind those big, beautiful eyes.

It wasn't until dessert was served that she smiled. A genuine one anyway. And that was thanks to Alice. Ever the entertainer.

"So I went over to Sam's the other day," Alice started but was soon cut off by Sam herself.

"Oh my God, Ali, is this about the jeans again?"

"It's weird!" Alice exclaimed.

"It's not!"

"Yeah, it is. What kind of psycho spends a relaxing day at home … in jeans?"

Lily and Ivy both giggled as Sam, clearly offended, huffed and crossed her arms defensively.

"They're comfy." She grumbled under her breath.

"No, they're fucking not. I'm gonna buy you some stretchy arse pants, girl, and you're never ever, *ever* gonna look back. Trust me. Elastic is your friend."

Relieved to see Ivy start to relax beside him, Ace drowned out the rest of the conversation and looked around the table. Everywhere he looked he saw men in love. Duke had tucked a sulky Sam to his side and was currently dotting her forehead with kisses. Jake had scooted closer to Lily and was lightly caressing her shoulders. And finally, his best friend, Brady, was chuckling right along with his wife, Ali. But it wasn't just amusement he had in his eyes, it was pure devotion.

When he twisted to look at a still giggling Ivy, something inside of him clicked. This was it. This was what it felt like to love someone. To realize that you would do anything within your power to make that person happy. To keep that smile on that person's face. Forever. That was how he felt right now. And how he knew he was madly, deeply, head over heels, crazy in love with Ivy.

CHAPTER THIRTEEN

Ivy had been avoiding Ace since the dinner party. When they'd returned home, they hadn't made love and she'd refused to tell him what was on her mind. Despite lengthy badgering. She'd snuck out of bed earlier than usual this morning and commenced chores on her own before locking herself away in her office.

Thankfully Ace had got the message loud and clear and was giving her some space. She knew she was being a bitch, but she needed to decompress. Seeing the way Ace held Hayley last night. The way he looked at her. Smiled at her. Rocked her. She thought she was going to throw up. She was in too deep. Way over her head. She was falling hard and fast for this man. And she knew if she didn't get out now, he had the ability to break her heart beyond repair.

Ace deserved everything. She knew that without a shadow of a doubt. But she also knew she couldn't give it to him. She'd never thought much about having kids herself. With her fertility issues and severe lack of a relationship for most of her life, she'd known for a while it wasn't meant to be. And that was okay. Well, it was. Until now.

"Urgh. Fuck my life." She let her head drop to the desk as she remained slouched over.

What was she going to do? The thought of ending things with Ace was making her stomach roil, but what choice did she have? Let things go further, let their feelings go deeper, and then what? Turn around one day and tell him she couldn't give him the life he so clearly wanted?

In an ideal world, she would just talk to him. Lay her cards on the table. Tell him what was possible and what wasn't. But she knew Ace; he was a good man. The type of man who always does the right thing. And in this case, sticking by her would be "the right thing." Settling. Living a life without the children of his own that he so badly wants. All because of her. She couldn't do that to him. She wouldn't. He'd been through enough as it was. He shouldn't have to compromise.

So, what do I do?

That was the million-dollar question. One she had to answer sooner rather than later. Her heart was already compromised. She'd never felt this way about anyone before. So the longer she ignored the problem, the harder she was going to fall. And the harder she fell, the more losing Ace would hurt like hell.

"Knock, knock!" Ace bellowed before cracking the door to her office slightly.

She gestured him in and let her eyes roam over him. He was perfect. Tall, strong, rugged. And giving her his signature look that never failed to make her melt.

"You okay, sugar?"

No. "Yeah. Of course. Why wouldn't I be?"

Ace raised an eyebrow at her. "Really? Is that why you've been avoiding me all day?"

She let out a small sigh. "I've just been busy, Ace, that's all."

"That's not all. You weren't okay last night, and you're not okay today. Talk to me, baby. If anything is worrying you, whether it's the ranch or *us* … we can work through it together. I swear."

Apparently she'd found the only emotionally available

man in Montana. One who wanted to talk to her about her feelings. Make things better. Was concerned about her. He really needed to stop making her fall harder for him. This was hard enough as it was.

"Really, honey, I'm okay. I'm just tired."

Ace frowned, clearly not believing her. She was at a loss. Lying was not her strong suit, and the idea of lying to Ace left a bad taste in her mouth. But she wasn't ready to tell him the truth just yet. She wasn't ready to give him up.

Rising from her swivel chair, she rounded the desk and walked straight into his arms.

One last kiss. One last day together. One last night. She'd be brave tomorrow.

***

Ivy's time was up. She'd savored every second of the last twenty-four hours and committed everything about Ace to memory.

She'd already decided not to tell him about her fertility issues. It wasn't fair on Ace. He deserved to have everything he ever wanted out of life. He shouldn't have to go without because of her. And that's exactly what he'd do. It was best he didn't know. Not now. Not ever.

Not being able to tell him the real reason she needed to end their relationship was probably going to be harder than telling him the truth though. She hated lying, but she had no other choice.

After cursing a blue streak under her breath, Ivy reached into the kitchen cupboard and grabbed hold of the Jack Daniels. Pouring herself an overly generous shot, she quickly downed it before Ace arrived back. She needed some liquid courage. Or any courage at all. She still didn't know how she was going to be able to look him in the eye and tell him she didn't want him.

Maybe I can look at the floor. Or focus on a spot behind him.

She still hadn't decided when Ace snuck up behind her

and wrapped his strong arms around her middle. She wished they could stay like this forever. Inhaling the familiar notes of sandalwood and musk for one last time, she reluctantly wiggled out of his hold and turned to face him.

"Have you been drinking?" One side of his mouth quirked up and revealed a crooked smile.

Damn, he's sexy. Shit. Stop looking at his mouth, Ivy, and fucking focus.

"We need to talk."

"Uh-oh. Sounds serious." The smile was still there. It was a crying shame that it wouldn't be for much longer.

Ivy took a step back and ignored the heart palpitations. "Seriously, Ace, we need to talk."

Picking up on her tone, all playfulness was now gone. "Okay … so talk." His arms were crossed now, and he looked ready for battle.

"I, uh, I don't think this is working out." It turns out she was right; she couldn't look him in the eyes. Her gaze immediately dropped to the floor. "I think maybe we should break up."

She saw his boots move toward her until she was backed up against the kitchen sink. He had other plans when it came to eye contact. Within seconds, his finger was under her chin and tilting her face upward. She swallowed her gasp as she got a first look at the hurricane of emotions flitting across Ace's handsome features. Pain. Anger. Confusion.

"What the hell are you talking about, Ivy?"

She swallowed down the nausea threatening to make its way up. "Us. Me, you. It's not working out. I can't do this anymore." Again, she focused on anything but those deep blue pools, her eyes darting to every other part of his face.

"Since when?" He'd dropped his finger, but he was still too close for comfort.

"Since now, Ace. Please don't make this harder than it already is."

"I don't understand, Ivy. What happened? What did I do? Please look at me, sugar. Please."

The desperation in his voice was almost her undoing, but she had to be strong. For Ace. It was the right decision. He deserved it all. Everything. This had to end now, before they both fell deeper. One day he'd thank her for this.

With a gentle shove of his chest, he jolted back. It was her turn to beg. "Please, Ace. I've made my decision. We're over."

"So that's it? No fighting for what we have. No talking about what's going on. No explanation whatsoever. Don't you think I deserve to know why, Ivy? 'Cause *I* fucking do."

This was the hard part. She was hoping not to stoop to this level. Taking a deep breath, her heart squeezed. She knew there was no going back after this. But it was the only way. He wasn't going to give up otherwise. He'd said as much. "I don't love you, Ace," she blurted, "and I never will."

She chanced a squinted glimpse at him and the pain she saw in his eyes almost brought her to her knees. It was official. She was a monster.

It worked. Without a word, he moved quickly toward the stairs. But before she let him disappear, she shouted after him. He turned to look at her, not hiding the anguish seeping from every inch of him.

Her voice was trembling. In fact, everything was trembling. She was a wreck. "Um … you can stay in the cabin for as long as you need … but under the circumstances, I'm not sure we should carry on working together."

He simply shook his head and left her there. Alone. She supposed she should get used to it. This was her life now.

As much as Ivy wanted to huddle in the corner and lick her wounds, she knew she needed to get out of there. She couldn't watch him pack. Couldn't witness him leave. She was already questioning the state of her heart and whether it would ever recover. Watching him walk out the front door would be too much. The final nail in the coffin.

Picking her keys off the counter, she ignored the tears

dampening her cheeks and headed toward the door.

CHAPTER FOURTEEN

Ace felt the couch cushion bounce but didn't bother looking up as Brady settled next to him. It had been three days. Three long, gut-wrenching days of misery. Skin grafts had nothing on the pain Ivy had the power to inflict on him.

"I'm heading into town. Why don't you come with me …? We could grab a drink at Mickey's, maybe shoot some pool … what do you think?"

Ace only grunted in response. There was no way in hell he was leaving this couch. Not for the foreseeable future anyway. He hadn't even dragged his ass upstairs to Brady and Alice's guest room to sleep. So he certainly wasn't about to go outside.

"Come on, man, just for a couple of hours. It will give Ali a chance to fumigate the sofa." His friend was clearly trying to lighten the mood. But right now, Ace didn't know if he'd ever smile again.

Instead of replying, Ace picked up his beer and took another swig. He needed to be numb.

It wasn't until Brady snatched the bottle right out of his hand that he finally acknowledged his friend. With a scowl.

"What the hell, man?"

"Well, fuck me, he talks," Brady drawled. "I was

beginning to wonder if Ivy didn't stop at the heart and ripped out your vocal cords too."

"Ha fucking ha. Now hand me back my beer."

"No. This has gone on long enough, brother. Three days, man. *Three days* you've been sat on my couch drowning your sorrows, grunting your replies. Well, enough. We're gonna talk. And use actual words. After that, you're gonna get your ass upstairs and in the fucking shower. And only then will I consider handing you back your beer."

Ace should have known Brady would only wait so long before riding him. Really, Ace was lucky he'd been left to his own devices for three whole days. But now his time was up. He just wished he'd finished his beer before having this conversation.

"Fine. You wanna talk? So talk." Ace slumped back into the fabric cushion and waited for the inevitable questions.

"You gonna tell me what happened with Ivy?"

"You know what happened. She broke up with me."

"Yeah. That, I got. What you didn't tell me though was why. Last I heard … and saw … you were sickeningly loved up. You have a fight or something?"

Ace ran a hand through his messy hair. It needed a cut. And a wash. There was no doubt he looked as shit as he felt. "No. Things were going well. Then all of a sudden she breaks it off. Tells me she doesn't love me and never could. Probably realized that I'm a fucking freak. Took her long enough."

"Jesus, man, first of all, you're not a fucking freak. Secondly, that doesn't make sense. You guys were all hot and heavy. I know, because the sight of you two going at it has been burned into my goddamn retinas. It just doesn't make sense that you go from that to this overnight. You sure nothing happened in the past week? Think, man."

Ace had been thinking. That's all he'd been doing. And he'd come up with nothing. Nothing at all. They hadn't so much as uttered a harsh word to each other, even in jest.

"I'm drawing a blank." He sighed as he dragged his hand

across his stubble. "I thought everything was fine. That morning we even …" He trailed off.

"Even what?"

He shot his friend a look. He wasn't going to say it out loud. Luckily, Brady understood immediately and nodded.

"Well, brother, if I wasn't convinced before that something else is at play here, then I am now. Women don't just go from breaking in the bed to breaking up in the space of a couple of hours. Not unless something happened."

Brady was right. No. They didn't.

***

Ace hadn't slept. Brady's words were niggling him. Something wasn't right. After the breakup it had been all too easy to fall into self-deprecation. It had become second nature to him ever since that one faithful day in the sandbox. Too easy to believe Ivy could never fall for a freak like him. But his friend was correct. Women don't just go from all in to all out without a valid reason.

Feeling restless and determined for some answers, he could barely remember the drive over to Moonrock. He definitely didn't remember changing out of his sweats. Not that it did him much good. Apparently four days of not shaving was all it took for him to take the disheveled look to a whole new level.

Running a hand nervously through his messy hair, he was painfully aware of the fact he still hadn't knocked. As soon as he'd jumped from his truck, his body had started pacing up and down Ivy's yard like some sort of wild animal.

Why hadn't he knocked yet? He'd initially told himself it was because he needed more time to figure out what to say to her. But the truth was, he was scared. Scared of hearing those words again. Scared it would shatter what was left of his heart.

"Ace." His name on her sweet lips twisted his insides. "W-what are you doing here?" He didn't miss the trepidation in her voice, or the heavy rise and fall of her chest as he turned to face her.

Her hair was gathered into a messy knot at the top of her head. And her usual jeans had been replaced with stretchy black yoga pants. As heavenly as her curves looked wrapped up in those clingy pants and a hole-ridden band T-shirt, he hadn't missed the dark circles under her eyes. She looked tired. Was it possible she hadn't been sleeping either?

It's because we belong together. Curled up in each other's arms.

"We need to talk."

She flinched at his hardened tone. Good. She needed to know he was serious about getting answers.

"There's nothing else to say," she whispered, letting her gaze drop to her feet.

He moved closer, but as soon as the scent of honey and jasmine made its way down his throat, he came to an abrupt halt. He missed waking up to that smell. Waking up to that taste.

"Why, Ivy? Just tell me why." His voice was thick with emotion. He couldn't hide it.

"I told you." Her voice was barely audible.

"The real reason, Ivy," he demanded. "Don't you think you owe me that at least?"

Ivy's head snapped up, her wide eyes giving her away.

I knew it. I fucking knew it.

Realizing her mistake, she quickly took a step back and dropped her head once again. "I already told you, Ace. Please don't make me say it again." Her voice shook as she pleaded. He really didn't want to hear her say those words again, but he needed to know the truth. Hell, he deserved it.

"That's bullshit and you know it." He regretted his harsh tone as soon as he saw Ivy's fingers tremble at her sides. Pushing down the urge to pull her into his arms and soothe her, he instead dared to take a step closer and gentled his voice. "We had something, Ivy. Something real. We still do, damn it. People don't just wake up one day and change their feelings. Change their heart. What did I do? Tell me, baby, please. I'll fix it. I promise. I'll do anything. Just tell me what I can do. Please."

A clog of emotion tightened his throat as he searched the features he could make out with her face still tilted downward. When her chin lifted slightly and he got a glimpse of fresh tears glistening in her eyes, it felt like a bullet to the chest. This time when she spoke, her gaze was locked on him.

"I can't do this. I can't be with you. It won't work. *We* won't work. We can't. I can't give you what you need. It's better to end this now before it's too late. Trust me. Please, Ace, please don't do this. It hurts too much." Her eyes pleaded just as fiercely with him. Melting his insides. She knew he could never deny her. Or stand by while she was hurting. She was using his weakness for her against him. "Please go ... please, Ace. I'm begging you."

A single curse left his mouth. He couldn't watch her cry. He couldn't be the reason for her tears. It hurt too much. She was begging him to go. Literally. As much as he wanted to push her. Make her tell him. She wasn't ready. And he couldn't risk her hurting even more than she already was.

Even though it pained him, he backed away. His eyes still trained on her, even while climbing into his truck. She was frozen in place on the doorstep. Her breathing just as tortured and ragged as his.

As he started the engine and tore his eyes from the woman he loved, he reminded himself of one thing. This was not the end. He still may not know the real reason for her ending things, but that didn't matter anymore. Not now that he'd seen her. Now he knew she was hurting just as badly as he was. Her feelings hadn't just disappeared overnight. They were still alive and kicking. And that gave him hope. All was not lost.

***

For the first time in a week, Ace had left the safety of

Brady's house and ventured into town. He'd finally gotten his appetite back and Dotty's diner was calling him. Sadly, he didn't even make it to the door before he was unceremoniously yanked into a familiar alley.

It wasn't a gentle yank either. No. It was violent. And pretty damn rude. Unfortunately, he knew exactly who had grabbed him even before he was hurtled against the cold brick and gripped rather harshly by the throat.

"Something on your mind, Teddy?" Ace deadpanned.

"I warned you. You hurt her and I hurt you." Teddy let out an animalistic growl. The man was actually baring his teeth at him.

He should probably be worried about the certain beating Ivy's brother was about to dole out. But he couldn't seem to make himself care. You never know, maybe it would make him feel something other than broken for a bit.

"Oh yeah? And I suppose the fact *she* broke up with *me* makes no difference?"

Teddy's eyes narrowed on him; Ivy clearly hadn't shared that particular detail with him. "I'm sure you deserved it." He grunted.

Ace let out a humorless laugh, making the fingers around his throat twitch. "Oh, yeah, I deserved it all right. I was a real fucking bastard ... buying her gifts, taking her out, helping her with the business, complimenting her, listening to her, caring for her, loving her ..." The bitterness was hard to hide as he spat the words in Teddy's face. "I totally deserved having my heart ripped right out with no explanation whatsoever."

They stared at each other in silence. Tension thickening the air as they both continued to snarl.

Finally, Teddy dropped the hold on his throat and took a step back, his intense green eyes not leaving Ace.

"She's a fucking wreck." Those words wounded worse than any punch. "You really have no idea why she broke up with you?"

Ace couldn't blame Teddy for being suspicious. If the

roles were reversed, Ace was sure he would have assumed the same. But the idea of Ivy being a wreck didn't sit well.

"No fucking clue, man. One minute we're good, the next she's ending it. She ever done this before … like with past relationships?"

"What other relationships?" Teddy looked at him like he was insane. "You're it. She's dated before, a while back, nothing serious though. You and her, that's the first relationship she's been in since high school."

What?

Suddenly Ace was finding it hard to breathe. He didn't know whether to fist-pump the air and rejoice in the fact he was her first relationship. Or shake her brother down and scream, "What the actual fuck?" How could the most beautiful woman, inside and out, not have been snapped up before? Or ever. Luke can't have been the only red-blooded male sniffing around her. It wasn't possible.

Maybe she just wasn't interested. It's not like you're Mr Relationship yourself.

That's when it clicked. They were the same. With no relationship experience, neither of them knew what the hell they were doing.

"Fuck." Teddy studied Ace as he rubbed the constant ache in his chest. "I love her, man. I really fucking love her. I don't know what to do."

After a long, slow breath, Ivy's brother's shoulders relaxed. Looks like Ace wasn't getting the shit kicked out of him today after all.

"You told her … that you love her?"

"She won't talk to me long enough for me to. And it's not the kinda thing I'd wanna say over the phone—even if she was taking my calls."

"I was really looking forward to kicking your ass." The big man huffed.

"Yeah, well, the way I'm feeling … I probably would've let you."

"Let me?" Teddy arched an eyebrow.

"Yeah, Navy boy, let you."

Teddy's deep laugh echoed around the alley, and for the first time in a week, Ace cracked a smile.

CHAPTER FIFTEEN

How many Cheetos is too many Cheetos?

As always, Ivy was pondering the most important questions.

It had been eight days, seven hours, and forty-two minutes since she'd dropkicked her own heart. And she wasn't doing well.

The outside world had officially become the enemy. After dodging calls from Ace, Alice, and Teddy, she'd eventually decided to turn off her phone. That was sometime during the day three mark. The only communication she'd allowed herself since then had been strictly work-related. And that took place in the safety of her office. On the landline or via email.

There was also that impromptu visit from Ace himself on day four. That had been fun. If fun meant feeling like you've just swallowed a whole load of razor blades. Seeing him in real life had derailed any progress she thought she was making. Not that crying for three days straight in the fetal position was progress. But the four days following had been even worse. If that were possible. She hadn't been able to shake the sight of him out of her head. It was sadness, anger, and disappointment all mixed into one longing gaze.

Looking down at the Cheeto dust covering her black yoga pants, Ivy sighed. What she didn't do though was pretend she was going to do anything about it. What was the point? Why shouldn't the outside match the inside, right? There was a whole load of destruction inside of her, way worse than any Cheeto dust.

Reaching for another handful of cheesy goodness, she typed into the laptop balanced on her knees. Google was her first stop as she searched for Chances of getting pregnant PCOS.

Who knows how long she stared at the luminous screen. She clicked on article after article. She read medical papers, news stories, and endless personal accounts from women just like her. Trying to memorize the different types of medicine she could try, the tests she should take, and the questions she should ask her doctor. It wasn't until her living room was plunged into darkness that she realized just how long she'd been at it.

She'd researched the condition before, of course, when she was first diagnosed. But nothing like this. She'd never gone down a Google black hole quite so deep before. Yes, she'd known there was a chance. That a percentage of women with the condition could still conceive. But for some reason, the more she read today, the more hope flared. And the more hope flared, the more she started to second guess herself.

No. Snap out of it, Ivy. The older you get, the harder it is. Oh, and let's not forget you never bothered to treat your PCOS before. And a slim chance isn't a guarantee. What if you and Ace tried and you got his hopes up, only to shatter them? False hope is worse than no hope at all. Right?

Cheetos. She needed more Cheetos. After tossing her laptop on the cushion beside her, she reached for the foil packet and cradled it in her arms.

Hugging a bag of chips. Well done, Ivy. You've hit peak pathetic.

***

Two days later and Ivy was emotionally exhausted, and it was starting to catch up with her physically. She'd barely made it through morning chores, to the extent she was seriously considering hiring a ranch hand.

It also didn't help that every part of her morning routine now reminded her of Ace. Her thoughts would automatically drift to the barn wall where he'd pin her down and render her boneless with his talented tongue. To the tack room where she'd pounce on him from behind and he would capture her and spin her around. Or to the pasture where they would watch the sunrise side by side as they took the horses for a morning ride.

I miss him so much.

How was it possible to not feel even remotely better, even after ten whole days? Breaking up with Ace now was supposed to make things easier on both of them. This didn't feel easy.

Untying her braid, she stared aimlessly at the laptop on her desk as it powered on. The damn office reminded her of Ace too. The desk. This chair. The damn heater, which she broke so she could strut around in short shorts in front of him. Oh, and then there was the business itself. Mocking her. Thanks to Ace's help, they'd managed to turn Moonrock around and they were busier than they'd ever been. It was the reason she was sat there right now, working through the pain.

Ungrateful much?

"Urgh. Get. A. Fucking. Grip. Ivy." She let her head fall into her hands as she mentally fought back the tears threatening to spill.

The office door creaking open snapped her out of her fourth breakdown of the day. Whipping her head up, she was faced with the very three people she'd been avoiding.

"No!" Her eyes darted from Brady to Alice. "No!" Then her gaze landed on Teddy. "And hell no!"

She quickly rose and weighed her options. Could she

stealthily slip out the door and make a run for it?

They're blocking the only exit, you moron.

"Ivy." Teddy's deep voice boomed. "We've given you enough time. And since you won't answer your goddamn phone, you've left us with no other choice than to hunt you down."

She felt hunted all right. Her brother was one thing. But Ace's best friend and his wife was a little overkill.

"I can't do this." She started walking around the wooden table. Apparently, she was taking her chances at fleeing. "I'm sorry, but I can't."

Predictably, it was her brother who caught her arm just as she approached the door. *So close, yet so far.* But it was Alice who spoke this time.

"Please, Ivy. Just give us a minute, and then we promise to leave you be."

She couldn't help but snort. "You expect me to believe all three of you came here for a friendly one-minute chat?"

Brady cleared his throat. "We're just worried about you, Ivy. If you're half as bad as Ace, then you shouldn't be on your own right now."

"Is he ... h-how's he doing?"

God, she was a bitch. Hadn't he been through enough? And now here she was inflicting more pain on him.

"Not good." That statement surprisingly came from Teddy of all people. How the hell would he know? Her confused expression aimed in his direction obviously reflected just that as her question was soon answered. "I ran into him the other day. The man's a wreck. A bit like you."

"I'm not a wreck." Her weak protest wasn't fooling anyone as they continued to look at her like a wounded puppy. "I just ... I just—breakups are hard, okay? I need some time. We both do. Then it will be all right. We'll be all right."

"You sure about that?" Brady drawled.

No. "Yes. People break up. This is what it's supposed to feel like." She really hoped that was true. But people wouldn't say time heals all if it wasn't true. Would they?

"Can we talk? Alone." Alice. Her only real friend. Was this the part where they break up now too? Was she taking Ace's side?

With a simple nod, Teddy dropped his hold on Ivy and left the office, closely followed by Brady. Suddenly needing to sit, she went back to her position behind the desk and waited for Alice to take a seat in front of her.

"What happened, Ivy? Last time I saw you guys, you were sickeningly happy. Like proper vomit-inducing."

"Cut straight to the chase, huh?" Not that she was surprised.

"Yeah, well, I'm not exactly about to win any prizes for my subtlety." A mischievous grin lit up Alice's pretty features. Ivy could feel her own lips twitch at the sight of it.

"It's for the best, Ali. I did him a favor. Trust me."

She probably shouldn't have said that. If she thought Alice was curious before. Now she was practically salivating at the confirmation that there was more to this breakup.

"Ivy … you can't just say shit like that and not elaborate. Spill. Now."

She squirmed in her chair. She'd been second-guessing the decision to keep the reason to herself ever since her Google blackhole. It sucked not having anyone to confide in. Really, really sucked. This was what friends were for, right?

"If I tell you, will you promise not to tell Brady or Ace? I mean it, Ali. You can't say anything. This stays between us."

Alice let out a sigh. "I don't keep secrets from my husband, Ivy. But I can promise that it won't get back to Ace. Not if you don't want it to. Brady would not break my confidence."

Ivy was quiet for a while. No secrets between husband and wife. That sounded nice. She wondered if it would have been the same between her and Ace. She hadn't hidden anything from him while they were together. Well, apart

139

from this. The big proverbial elephant in the room that caused their breakup.

"Okay." Ivy fiddled with her fingers. "There's something that Ace doesn't know. Something that would no doubt break us up eventually. So, I did what I had to do and broke up with him now, before we both got in too deep. To lessen the pain, y'know?"

"Okay," Alice said slowly. "And that something is?"

"I-I can't have kids. Well … uh … I might not be able to have them. I have PCOS, polycystic ovary syndrome. And, well, I didn't think I'd ever meet anyone I'd want to … or even if I did, I didn't know if I'd even want kids … so it wasn't a big deal. But then I met Ace, and have you seen him with Hayley? Jesus, just the sight of him with that little girl squeezes my frickin' ovaries. And he wants kids. He should have kids—he'd be an amazing dad. Really fucking amazing. And y'know I want that for him. He deserves it. After everything he's been through, he really does. He deserves everything. And I probably can't give that to him. And that's not right, Ali. It's not okay, and I just … I just…"

Ivy's breathless babbling was soon cut off by Alice's firm hands on her shoulders, anchoring her.

When did she get up?

"Whoa, whoa, whoa." Alice pulled her into a hug she never knew she needed so badly. "It's okay. Shhh. Breathe. Just breathe, okay."

The dam broke and tears streamed down her cheeks. It felt so good to get that all out. Even if the delivery was a little clumsy. It felt like a weight off her chest. And to be hugged. Held. Comforted. She was so sick of doing everything for herself. She didn't want to be strong anymore. She couldn't. Not when she felt so utterly broken.

She didn't know how long she sobbed into her friends' arms. But it was long enough that her tears eventually dried. When Alice pulled back, she knew their conversation wasn't over. It was only just beginning.

***

Ivy hadn't been able to shake Alice's words.

She's wrong. It's too late.

After eating dinner alone. Again. She finished washing her solitary plate and placed it in the drying wrack. She then turned her attention to the drawer just to the side of the sink and slowly tugged it open. It was time. She'd faced Alice, Brady, and Teddy. She'd shared. She'd cried. And now she was going to put on her big girl pants and turn her phone on.

Taking a deep breath, she cradled the phone against her chest and headed back to the couch. Once she was safely tucked under her blanket, she held down the power button and waited.

It didn't take long for chimes to echo around the room. Through squinted eyes, Ivy took her first look at the screen. Her stomach lunged at just the sight of Ace's name. He'd tried to call her the first few days. He'd even sent her a message asking, no, pleading, with her to call him. But then he'd clearly stopped. Given up. The past few days she'd only had missed calls from Teddy and Alice. But there was a message from an unknown number. After clicking on the message, her mouth dropped open.

You okay, sweetie? Ace told me what happened. Just wanted to check on you and make sure you are all right. Let me know if you need anything. Liz x

Liz. Lovely, thoughtful Liz. Ivy had upped and dumped her son and yet sweet, sweet Liz was checking up on her. Ivy couldn't believe it. If she needed further proof that she didn't deserve Ace, this was surely it. This woman deserved grandchildren. Lots of them. To spoil, to love, to share that big heart with. Damnit. Just when she thought she was all out of tears, she sprang a leak.

She dropped the phone onto the cushion next to her and pushed it further away with her feet. Bad, bad phone. She needed to rip these big girl pants right off because ... fuck this.

A bang on her front door only made her grimace harder. Hadn't she had enough visitors today? There was no way in hell she was answering that door. No way.

CHAPTER SIXTEEN

Okay, so this wasn't the plan. Or a plan of any kind. But after hearing about Brady and Alice's visit or more likely ambush of Ivy today, he just couldn't help himself. If she was going to tell anyone what the hell was going on, then it was going to be him. No one else.

He banged again on Ivy's door. She was home. Her truck was here. The lights were on. And he could just feel her. Running his hand through his damp hair, he tried his hardest to control his breathing. He looked down at his attire and frowned. He should have thought this through. Everything had just happened so quickly. One minute he was stepping out of the shower, the next he was pulling on sweats and hightailing it over to Moonrock.

Banging his fisted hand a third time against the ancient wood, he let out a heavy sigh. Was she really going to ignore him like this? Just pretend she wasn't home?

"Open the door, Ivy. I know you're in there."

He heard a dainty little whimper through the wood. He knew it. But she still wasn't opening up.

Goddamnit. Desperate times call for desperate measures.

With a quick glance up at the bedroom window, he knew what he had to do. Ten days. He'd given her ten whole days.

Time was up. She was going to hear what he had to say. Whether she wanted to or not.

He'd managed to scale halfway up the drainpipe before she'd cottoned on to what was happening.

"What the actual fuck are you doing?" Ivy screeched.

The front door was now wide open and Ivy was glaring up at him. Arms crossed. Nose red and eyes puffy. Looking as cute as hell. Ace angled himself so he could stare down at her and couldn't help but smile, even as she continued to berate him.

"You're climbing up my drainpipe?"

"Yes, I am."

Green fire was shooting out of her narrowed eyes. "Why the hell are you climbing up my drainpipe, Ace?"

"You wouldn't let me in," he stated simply, still unable to wipe the smile off his face.

"So … what … you thought you'd just break in?"

"Yep."

It didn't exactly feel like it right now, but this was a victory. He didn't fancy squeezing his big ass body through the bedroom window anyway. With that in mind, he began his descent back down the pipe.

"*Yep! Yep!*" Ivy mimicked, getting more and more irritated the closer he got to her. "You don't just go breaking into people's houses, Ace. What kind of maniac climbs up a drainpipe when someone doesn't answer a door? Huh?"

It was clearly a rhetorical question. So he didn't answer.

"Have you ever thought that maybe if someone is home and doesn't answer the door it's probably because … oh I don't know … that person doesn't want to see you? And said person is not silently granting permission for you to break into their fucking house!"

Cute as hell.

Ace jumped the last foot and spun to face a still very angry Ivy. Immediately he noticed that she'd been crying. Jesus. He couldn't help himself. He reached out and cupped her cheek.

"Baby. What's wrong? Are you okay? Did you hurt yourself?"

That clearly wasn't the right thing to say. He watched as more tears prepared to stream. She shook her head but didn't reply.

"Talk to me, sugar, please." This time he pulled her into his arms. To his delight, she didn't protest and simply melted into his hold.

Not wanting to risk her pulling away, he didn't say anything else. Instead, he greedily inhaled her honey scent and memorized the way she felt pressed against his chest. Just in case this was his last chance to hold her. He'd missed the feel of her delicate fingers on his body, even if they did leave a trail of heat in their wake. And the feel of her long, wavy hair tickling his chin as she rested her head against the beating of his heart. She was perfection. This was perfection.

As she slowly pulled away, he reluctantly let her go. Instantly missing her. She belonged in his arms. Why couldn't she see that?

"You shouldn't be here," she whispered, avoiding looking him in the eye.

"I'm not going anywhere. Not until we've talked."

"There's nothing else to say."

"Yes, baby, there is." He took a tentative step closer. "Shall we go inside?"

"No."

"Okay, sugar." He couldn't go another moment without her looking at him. Letting his finger slip under her chin, he tilted her face until he was gazing into her. "You don't have to say anything, just listen to me, okay?"

Ivy trembled but kept her eyes on him as she nodded.

"I've never been good with words, so bear with me, okay?" He really wished he'd prepared something right about now, but he supposed speaking from the heart would work too. It would have to. "The first time I laid eyes on you, I knew you were special. And it wasn't just because you were the most beautiful woman I've ever seen … no. I mean, you are, but you also had this sort of quiet strength about you, an inner beauty that just made you glow … like some sort of angel." He ignored Ivy's sharp inhale and continued. "And then when I heard about the ranch … the thought of you running this place all by yourself … it gutted me. Fucking gutted me. I'd known you less than five minutes and all my instincts were screaming at me to protect you, look after you, make you mine. Just the thought of you being anything less than okay was unacceptable. I should have known then. I really should have. But that doesn't matter, no, it doesn't, 'cause I know now."

His breath was feeling heavier with every exhale. Especially after he'd noticed a sheen of moisture beginning to glisten in Ivy's eyes. The last thing he wanted was to make her cry again, but he needed to get this out. She'd gone too long without hearing it.

"Know what?"

"That you're it for me, Ivy. You're the one."

"Ace … you can't. No … you need to stop, please. Please—"

His big hands trembled as they surrounded her face. "I'm in love with you, Ivy. I fucking love you. Do you hear me? I'm yours. You own me. Tell me what I can do to fix this. Please. I'll do anything; I swear to God. Anything. I can't fucking live without you, baby."

He didn't hide his pain. He let her see it all. Even the matching tears that were readying to cascade down his cheeks.

"No, no, no … you can't love me. No. I can't … you deserve more. You deserve everything, Ace. I can't give you that … don't you see?" She furiously shook her head. She wasn't making any sense.

Seconds later she was running inside, but he wasn't letting her run away again. He followed her and edged inside the door before she had a chance to shut it.

"No more running, Ivy. Tell me. Tell me why. If I

deserve everything, then I deserve that. Don't I?"

Crowding her against the wall in the hallway, he waited for her breathing to even out. She was shaking. Scared. All he wanted to do was pull her back into his arms and tell her everything was going to be okay. But he resisted. He needed to hear the truth.

"I can't give you the life you want." Her voice was quiet and shaking just as much as her body.

"And what life is that, Ivy?"

"Children." *What?* "You want kids, right?"

"Sure. I guess. But what does that have to do with anything?"

"I have PCOS."

"Okay ..." Was he supposed to know what that was? "And?"

"And it means ... it's likely I won't be able to have kids. You want children and there's a ... there's a chance I can't give you that, Ace."

That's what this has all been about? Jesus fucking Christ.

"Do you want kids, sugar?" He made sure his voice was calm, hoping it would rub off on a now panting Ivy.

"I didn't, but then ... then I met you and I thought about having kids with you, and suddenly it was all I could think about. All I wanted. And you'd be such a good dad. I know it. And I can't ... I can't give you that. You should have that. You should, Ace. You should have everything. Even if it means we can't be together. If I keep you, then there's a chance that you wouldn't be able to have that, and that would be selfish of me." Tears dripped off her face and onto the floor. Every drop tearing his heart apart even more. "I can't do that to you. I won't. There's that saying, y'know the one. If you love something, set it free. That's what I have to do, Ace. For you. For us."

"If it comes back, it's yours." His voice was gruff, and he was struggling to see through his own misty eyes.

"What?"

"The saying, sugar. *If you love something, set it free. If it comes back, it's yours.* Well, I came back. I'm yours, Ivy. And if you think for one second that I'm going anywhere after you've just admitted that you love me, then you're shit out of luck."

"Ace—"

"No. It's my turn to speak. Look, I'm not gonna pretend I know what the hell PCOS is, but if it means we can't have a baby the old-fashioned way, then who the fuck cares?! You want kids, Ivy? I'll give you kids. We'll try IVF or get a surrogate or adopt or foster. It doesn't matter. What matters is that we do it together. 'Cause I can't have a family without you—wanna know why?"

He watched as Ivy bit down on her bottom lip, waiting for him to carry on.

"'Cause *you* are what's gonna make it a family. You as my wife. You as the mother to my children … no matter how they come about. You as the woman I wanna spend the rest of my life with. Don't you get it, Ivy? I don't want anyone else. I told you before, and I'll tell you again, you're *it* for me."

He couldn't wait any longer. Lowering his head, he quickly captured her lips. He tasted the salt on his tongue as he ran it along the seam. As soon as she opened for him, he knew he was home. As their tongues tangled, his heart raced and hope bloomed. She was kissing him back.

When she started to pull away, he clung to her face and kept her close.

"I love you, Ace. You're it for me too. I think that's why it hurt so much to let you go. But you have to be sure. I mean it. If you think you'll change your mind about me, you have to tell me now. I don't think I'd survive another breakup. I really don't."

She loves me. She really loves me.

Ace dropped to his knees. "Marry me?"

"What? Ace, get up! Stop being ridiculous!"

"Marry me, Ivy?" he repeated. "I'm not fooling around. I love you. You love me. Make me the happiest man alive and marry me?"

"You're insane!" Ivy began to pelt him on the shoulder, and he could feel his mouth widen into a grin.

"Insanely in love. Say you'll marry me, Ivy?"

He kept his balance as he felt another hard shove against his shoulder. "This is not fucking funny, Ace!"

Cute as hell.

EPILOGUE

Ivy struggled out of the leather armchair. An involuntary groan slipped past her lips as she unceremoniously flung herself up the rest of the way.

"Hey, sugar." Ace winked as he tore off his jacket. "You're looking especially beautiful today."

She huffed as she snaked a hand around to support her lower back. "Don't sugar me. I'm nauseous and tired, and I'm pretty sure I hate you."

Ace's sexy smirk only grew wider. How freaking annoying. How was it fair that the man got sexier with age, and she just got wider?

"You want me to make you a ginger tea, baby? Why don't you sit back down, and I'll get you one, yeah?"

Damn, it was hard to stay mad at him. Even though it was all his fault she was in this state. "I have to go up and check on Cici, make sure she's awake, or she won't sleep tonight."

Ivy watched as Ace expertly crossed the toy minefield that was now their living room and wasted no time pulling her into his arms.

"I'll check on Cici and you sit that pretty little butt down and wait for me to bring you ginger tea. Then I'll get started on dinner. How does that sound, huh?"

"Why are you being so nice to me? I just told you I hate you." She nestled her head into his chest, absorbing the comfort. Maybe she just needed a hug.

Her husband's fingers trailed up and down her spine. "You get a free pass, sugar. You're the one carrying our little peanut, not me."

This peanut was anything but little. She was kicking Ivy's ass. Literally. For a tiny baby, she kicked like she was holding a grudge. And don't get her started on all the pregnancy myths she'd spent the past six months busting. It only took her a day to work out that the pregnancy glow everyone talks about was just sweat. She was also delighted to discover morning sickness was an all-damn-day and all-damn-pregnancy kind of thing.

She snuggled deeper into Ace's chest. "Okay. I should get some perks I guess. Growing a baby inside of me and all that." She smiled into the vibrations as he let out a chuckle.

The truth was, as uncomfortable as pregnancy was, she couldn't be happier that they were adding to their little family. Two years ago, after undergoing the adoption process, they'd been blessed with Cici. And she was perfect. Even at only five years old, Ivy already knew she was going to make the best big sister.

Ace reluctantly released his hold of her and brushed his lips over hers. "Mmm, not only does my wife get prettier and prettier each day, she also tastes just like honey. I'm one lucky man." He went back for another taste. "How 'bout an early night tonight, sugar?"

She could feel her cheeks heat. How was it that after five years, he could still make her blush?

"I'll think about it."

"You do that."

He dipped down for one last kiss before heading for the stairs. Before she sat down again, she thought really long and hard about whether she needed to pee. No. Not right now, not even a tiny bit.

Just as she was angling her body back into the armchair, the doorbell rang.

Yes! Good timing. I'm still upright. One second later and they'd have to wait a hell of a long time.

Waddling down the hallway, she swung the door open to find Alice grimacing. She too had a matching belly. And waddle. Apparently both Brady and Ace had been bringing their A-game six months ago.

"You okay, Ali?"

"Stupid frigging heartburn. I keep thinking I'm having a bloody heart attack." Not waiting for an invitation, Alice waltzed in and headed in the direction of the couch.

Ivy followed behind, giggling. "I'm still switching between wanting to throw up and wanting to eat everything in sight."

"Oh, I'm pretty much eating enough for a family of five right now." She paused in her strides to ponder her own statement. "Maybe that's why I have heartburn. Huh." Then she was back on the move.

Once they'd both double checked neither of them wanted to pee, they sank into the couch cushions.

"So, not that it's not nice to see you, but what do I owe this pleasure?" Ivy twisted to face her friend.

"I missed you."

"You did?" She brightened.

Alice and Ivy had grown even closer over the years. And thanks to Ace and Brady's bromance, they spent most weekends together. It had been at least a week since they'd all gotten together though. It was good to know she wasn't the only one missing her friend.

"Hell yeah, I did. There is way too much testosterone at home. I need an estrogen fix."

"Y'know, I'm not sure Kyle can be included in your testosterone fest. He's only two years old!"

"Yeah, yeah." Alice waved her off. "Whatever. I'm

outnumbered. Two penises to one. And when this little guy pops out, it's gonna be three to one. Three to one, Ivy! Not cool."

Cici came barrelling down the stairs at that moment, followed closely by Ace.

"Hey, Ali, what brings you over?" Ace rumbled.

Cici threw her arms out at Ivy's feet, waiting for help climbing up onto her mom's lap. She was such a cutie. Snuggling up with her little girl, she let Ace and Alice catch up while she savored her cuddles.

When she tuned back into the conversation, it became apparent that no one would be having an early night tonight.

"No need to cook. Brady and Jake are in town right now picking up a fuckload of food. Oh, and they're gonna invite Sam, Duke, and little Lola too. Lily's got Kyle, and she'll be over with Hayley and Harry in about an hour. And I think Teddy and Summer said they'll be popping by as well."

"Oh, and talking of Teddy and Summer," Alice continued as her attention went back to Ivy, "she was telling me the other day about how they wanted to take on another construction project. *Another one!* Those two are fricking crazy. I mean, goddamn certifiable! Mind you, nothing should surprise me when it comes to them. No matter how much I wanted to … *even I* didn't resort to chucking whiskey bottles at Brady's head when he drove me crazy."

Ivy laughed right along with her friend, but the smile on her face never faded. This was her family. The one Ace and she had made together. She wasn't alone anymore, that was for sure. And she never would be again.

SEE WHERE THE BLUESTONE SERIES BEGAN:

Love Tools

What happens when the king of casual meets the queen of picking the wrong men?

Lily is running. From a dead-end job, a neurotic mother and all the losers she dared to date. Moving halfway across the world to Bluestone County seemed like a good idea at the time. So did reopening her estranged father's hardware store. But now she isn't so sure.

Small town living has its perks though. Wide-open space, clean air, and sexy cowboys. Well, one sexy cowboy. Jake. Who also just so happens to be the new bane of her existence. At least when he's not talking, she can admire the view.

Jake is the king of casual. The love of his life has always been his ranch, and that was fine with him. He never really saw the point in long-term. But all that changes when a mouthy, blonde sasses him into oblivion. He should have known she'd be trouble as soon as he laid eyes on her. Now it's too late. She's all he can think about. All he has to do is convince her that he's finally the right man.

Isobel Reed's hilarious, emotionally charged romance will have you holding your side with laughter or reaching for a tissue. Reminiscent of small-town romance by Tessa Bailey or Kristen Ashley, you will fall in love with LOVE TOOLS and Isobel Reed's unique writing style.

EXCERPT

Lily took the opportunity to scan his face and let her eyes wander down him. His broad shoulders filled out his check shirt that pulled tight across his muscled chest. She tried her hardest not to gawk as her gaze travelled down farther to his mud-stained denim jeans that moulded perfectly to tensed thighs.

Holy shit, he's hot. Do all the men in Montana look like this?

"You about done checking me out, darlin', or do you want me to turn around and show you the back?"

She felt her cheeks flame as her eyes flicked back up and she caught sight of his cocky grin. Before she could attempt to deny what she'd been doing, his expression turned more serious as he gave her a once-over. "I didn't know Matt had a daughter."

Surprise, surprise.

"No shit. He wasn't exactly father of the year."

Lily couldn't help but think of the irony. Her father had become friends with some guy young enough to be his son, yet he still couldn't quite be bothered to pick up the phone and call his own daughter.

Marlboro Man's smile became crooked as his glare intensified. "You always swear like a trucker, darlin'? Here I thought English women were all class and manners."

Is he being fucking serious?

She let out a huff; she couldn't believe the nerve of this guy. "I'm sorry, have I stepped into the past? Are you gonna ask me why a little woman like me isn't married next?"

"All right, sweetheart, calm down." He sniggered, clearly

amused by the steam coming out of her ears.

Expiry Dating

Sparks start more than a fire... They start an explosion.

Alice is not happy. Her ex screwed her over, literally. One day her mother is dreaming of a white wedding, the next, Alice is hurling hardbacks at a naked boyfriend caught in bed with her best friend. So she did the only logical thing she could think of. She got the hell out of there. In fact, she left the country.

It's not long before she discovers the perks of small-town living, and she even finds herself a job. There is just one thing stopping this all from being perfect though. One infuriating person she just can't seem to shake. Brady Mitchell. It figures that the hottest man she's ever seen also just so happens to be the most annoying one on the planet.

Brady is back home and trying to come to terms with life outside the military. Adjusting to a new job and new limitations from his injury, he expected to settle into a slower pace of life, maybe even a quiet one. That was until Alice Hart came bulldozing into his world. The woman was anything but quiet. Loud, angry and sexy as hell, yes. But definitely not quiet.

Alice and Brady ignite inside and outside the bedroom. But will they survive the burn?

EXPIRY DATING- the second book in the Bluestone Series is a funny, wild romp along the lines of Stephanie Berget's cowboy romances or Sarina Bowen's True North series. EXPIRY DATING features a retired marine and the feisty young woman who steals his heart. While it is a part of a series, Expiry Dating can be read as a standalone. Grab your copy today.

EXCERPT

There he was—Brady—all six foot two of him. The new bane of her existence. He was wearing a fitted, tan, cop uniform so sexy it should be illegal. If she didn't already know he was the devil, she could easily be fooled by his dark, brooding good looks. Even his damn caramel-coloured eyes were mesmerizing.

Mesmerizing eyes? Get a frigging grip, Alice. He's the devil, remember?

It had been two weeks since they'd met in Vegas at Lily and Jake's impromptu wedding, and despite trying to avoid Brady like the plague since then, he just kept showing up. Yes, Bluestone was small, and Alice was staying at his best friend's ranch, but it was actually getting ridiculous. He was everywhere. Whenever she ventured out, whether it was to get coffee or go shopping, he was there, waiting in the shadows, ready to make her life miserable.

"Looking good, sweetness." Brady smirked as he purposely knocked her on the way over to the fridge, where he swiftly removed a beer bottle.

Alice shot him a glare over her shoulder. "Wish I could say the same to you, Brady, but it appears as if the rumours really are true and beer does go straight to a man's gut."

She was lying, of course. There was no beer belly in sight. The man was a wall of solid muscle, but something about him drove her absolutely insane. It apparently also meant she couldn't control her mouth whenever he was in the vicinity. He'd somehow managed to crawl under her skin in a matter of minutes of them meeting, and insults had been hurled between them ever since.

Brady's silky laughter bellowed behind her. "You offering to help me work it off, sweetness?"

NOW AVAILABLE IN EBOOK AND PRINT
WHERE BOOKS ARE SOLD

ISOBEL REED

DON'T MISS THE FOURTH BOOK IN THE BLUESTONE SERIES:

Love Shots

Chapter One

"What. The. Fuck. I can't believe you just threw a fucking lamp at me!" Teddy seethed, his voice getting louder and louder. "What the hell is wrong with you Summer?"

"*Me?*" Summer's hazel eyes narrowed on him as she easily matched his volume, "what the hell is wrong with *you?*"

A second later, something else was hurtling towards him and narrowly missing his head. An ear-piercing smash later, he spared a glance at the floor to his left and couldn't help but scowl. This had to be a bad dream. Dark liquid was now seeping into his hardwood floors while crooked shards of glass stood to attention.

"Have you lost your damn mind woman? That was an eight-hundred-dollar bottle of whiskey!"

"Oh no." She brought her chipped red nails up to her face to frame her mock shock expression. "Sucks when someone takes something that isn't theirs… doesn't it?"

"For the last goddamn time, Mickey wanted to sell, and I wanted to buy. End of story. You weren't in the country… you're never in the country! How on earth was I supposed to know Mickey promised you the bar? I'm not a damn mind reader Summer!"

Teddy mentally cursed himself. It was too late for this bullshit. Why did he have to go and answer the door? He was old enough and ugly enough to know that nothing good ever came from answering your door after midnight.

He certainly hadn't been prepared to see Summer Willis. It had been five long years since he'd seen the beautiful, blonde, pain in his ass. And now here she was, using the contents of his shelf and his living room wall for target practice.

After muttering some imaginative expletives under her breath, she took a step towards him. And then another. He finally had a chance to study her, something he hadn't been able to do since she'd barged her way into his apartment and started yelling. Something was off. The Summer he knew was always so put together. Composed. Perfect. Even when the words coming out of her pretty little mouth were anything but.

Errant strands of hair hung down from the messy knot at the top of her head. Her short sleeved blue blouse was slightly crumbled, and he noticed mud stains streaking the knees of her jeans. His eyes zeroed in on the skin above the black bracelets covering her wrist. It was bruised.

What the hell is that?

Before he had time to think, he was reaching for her arm to get a better look. "Who did this to you?" His forceful demand was a direct contradiction to the gentle way he circled her wrist as he held it up.

For a second, he saw sadness in those green-brown eyes. A rare display of vulnerability there and gone so fast, if he'd have blinked he would have missed it. Wrenching her hand back, her expression defaulted back to hard, "none of your business."

Teddy didn't think Summer noticed that she had just basically admitted to a person being responsible for that mark. But he had. And he wouldn't be forgetting any time soon. He wasn't about to push her for more information right now though. Not unless he wanted his apartment trashed even more than it already was.

"What can I do?" He kept his voice calm, even though he was feeling anything but. Someone had hurt Summer. His Summer.

"Give me back my bar." She retorted.

"You know I can't do that. I know you've not been back to Bluestone for a while but... ever since I left the Navy, Mickey's has come to mean a lot to me."

Her expression betrayed her again. Instantly going from rage to shock to concern at his revelation. "You left the Navy? Why? When?"

There she was. There was the woman he remembered. It was good to know she was still there. "Yeah dollface, I left. Three years ago. Moved back here. And your grandaddy set me up with a job at Mickey's and now... well, you know the rest."

"Don't think I missed you ignoring the *why* Teddy." The sass was back.

"That's right dollface. I am ignoring it. Because it's a long damn story and I'm too damn tired. So, if you're done redecorating my apartment," he gestured around the small dark room. Even more dark since she smashed one of the two lamps that he had. "I think it's time for me to head back to bed."

Summer gulped. How she could look both scary and vulnerable at the same time was a complete mystery.

"I need a job." She blurted. "I planned on working at Mickey's."

A laugh escaped before he had time to swallow it. "Jesus Christ Summer. This is how you ask me for a job? Barging in here at two AM, throwing my shit at me and calling me an asshole?"

The corner of her lips curved up into a smirk. He was reminded right then and there what a smile from Summer Willis could do to him.

COMING SOON!

ABOUT THE AUTHOR

Isobel was born and raised in London. She still lives along the River Thames with her husband and her substantial book collection. Ever the hopeless romantic, she fell in love with the genre from a young age and was inspired to write her own stories. When she's not feasting on romantic comedies or binge reading her hoard of contemporary romance novels, Isobel is writing.

https://www.facebook.com/isobelreedbooks
https://www.instagram.com/isobelreedbooks/
https://www.isobelreed.net/
https://www.amazon.com/author/isobelreed
https://www.goodreads.com/Isobel_Reed
https://www.bookbub.com/authors/isobel-reed